SAM CRESCENT AND STACEY ESPINO

EVERNIGHT PUBLISHING ®

www.evernightpublishing.com

Copyright© 2022

Sam Crescent and Stacey Espino

Editor: Audrey Bobak

Cover Artist: Jay Aheer

ISBN: 978-0-3695-0505-7

SAM CRESCENT AND STACEY ESPINO

THE BIKER'S PLAYTHING

Straight to Hell MC, 1

Sam Crescent and Stacey Espino

Copyright © 2022

Chapter One

"No, please, no!" The sound of the rat's squeal filled the air. Seeing as he was standing in his own grave, which Lord had made him dig himself, there was no one to hear.

"You defied our laws. I can't have that."

"I'm sorry, Lord. I didn't know what I was doing. It was a mistake. I'll do anything. I'm so sorry."

"Anything?" Lord asked.

"Yes. Please. Anything."

Lord smiled. "Kiss my feet."

"What?"

"You heard me. Kiss my fucking feet."

The hole was big enough for the rat to still reach his boots. He waited. As soon as his lips were close, Lord kicked out, hitting him hard in the face. The man fell back, cupping his jaw, blood flowing between his fingers.

His men all laughed.

They knew the moment a rat was declared, the only sure thing was death.

"Please, what about my daughter? She's not responsible. Please."

"Don't worry. Ally will get the right treatment owed to her by the club. You really should have thought about that before doing what you did." Pulling out his gun, which he only used to take out rats in the club, he fired one bullet, and it went straight through the man's head.

He was already in his grave and Lord nodded. Justice had been served. His men clapped their hands, all of them happy with the way this ended.

Brick, his VP, came to him, putting a hand on his shoulder. Lord didn't like to be touched and shrugged him off. The men knew not to put a hand on him.

"I want the cop next," Lord said.

The rat, Richard Prixman, had been an accountant of sorts, working at the club's strip joints. Not only had the son of a bitch been stealing from him, but he'd also decided to use their records to try to bring a case against the club. As if he'd ever allow that to happen.

The club was his life. He protected everyone.

"Get the prospects to clean this shit up." He kicked some mud at the dead face. "It's a shame we couldn't mount his head on a spike to serve as a warning to anyone tempted to turn their backs on us."

Leaving his mess behind, Lord made his way to the club. One of the club whores was at the bar, cleaning out a glass. He nodded for her to pour him a shot, which she did without question.

After knocking it back, he headed to the parking lot where his bike was ready and waiting.

"You're not going on your own," Brick said.

"This is my job."

"Take Reaper with you. I'll handle shit here."

He glared at Brick. "You think I need a babysitter?"

"No, but you do need someone to rein in your anger. Do as you're asked, please," Brick said.

Lord raised his brow.

Brick held his hands up. "I don't mean no disrespect. You know that."

"Do I? The way I see it, my VP thinks he can tell me what to do."

"Advise you. That's it. I don't want you to hurt yourself or worse, do something you might regret."

"He's right," Reaper said. "You fucking know it, boss."

He looked between his men. His temper was well known, especially when it came to defending the club, and right now, killing the rat hadn't satisfied his hunger. When one of his informants called a week ago, he thought it was a joke. It wasn't. Someone wanted to end his club, and it wasn't the first time. Between fighting for turf and ending clubs himself through wars, he was used to always looking over his shoulder. When it came to an insider willing to take on him and his club, well, he couldn't have that. The betrayal was too close to home, and it didn't help that it had been Richard Prixman. He'd helped that son of a bitch get the job and this was how he got repaid? He was pissed off. No, he was furious.

Usually, killing the person responsible for his shit mood helped to improve it, but it had only made him angrier. He was pissed off and ready to kill even more people.

"Then hurry the fuck up. We know this piece of shit is waiting at a barn out in the middle of nowhere. I don't have time to waste." He clicked his fingers. "Oh, and get the rat's daughter here too."

"You know Ally doesn't live with him. She declared emancipation from him when she was fifteen. The girl's been living on her own ever since," Brick said.

He didn't allow himself to get embroiled with his workers' business. Richard had issues, he got that, but didn't they all? As far as he was concerned, his only regret was not killing the daughter first, so the rat could have watched her die.

Every one of the men at the club had issues, but he didn't hold their hands or ask them about their problems. Instead, he liked to stick to the good, old, reliable method of not giving a shit.

"Just do it. You know how this works."

"Fine. We'll bring her in."

Climbing on his bike, he allowed the purr to sink into his senses. The scent of oil, the leather, the roar, it was all sweet magic, but it still didn't do enough to stem his need for blood. Gripping the handlebars, he revved the engine, not waiting for his enforcer to get ready. He was out of there. He didn't need a sitter.

Taking the open road, he knew this was where he belonged. For many years, he'd been wandering through life, fighting, hunting, and trying to find himself, when he discovered his place right here in this very club, Straight to Hell MC. It had once been owned by a man who went by King. He'd been the one to rule this place, to have his men bow down at his feet, but greed had set him on a path of destruction. If it hadn't been for Lord, they'd all be dead, rotting in their graves. Life had certainly taken a dramatic turn.

He hadn't been prepared to take care of these men, and yet, somehow, he'd managed. He'd been able to take the role of president, to remove all the men with King's influence, and now the club was exactly how he wanted it. Ruthless men who were one hundred percent loyal to the club, whose motives he didn't have to question. They would always have his back. And he'd die for them in return.

It didn't take long for Reaper to catch up with him. His enforcer was one hell of a rider and there was never going to be any way of getting shit past him.

Heading toward town, he noticed many people stopped to watch them. Whenever he decided to venture into town with the club to take care of business, most people tried to keep a wide berth from him. He didn't mind at all.

Having people near him put him on edge. He was always tempted to reach for his gun, to shoot without giving a fuck when someone pissed him off—that was just his prerogative. So, it was best to keep his distance.

The cop who dared to defy the club lived in a little farmhouse past the town, near a patch of open road. Pulling down the old dirt road, he arrived just in time to see the man himself scamper into his home.

Climbing off his bike, he didn't wait for Reaper. Instead, he barged into the house, grabbing the cop by the back of the neck and throwing him across the room. He landed against a ceramic urn that shattered.

"So, you think you can just take my money, and then turn rat on me?"

"No, please," the cop said.

Grabbing him by the hair, he dragged him outside, ready to kill him.

"Wait," Reaper said.

Lord held the gun up, ready to train it on Reaper. "You're sticking up for this piece of shit? Did you turn rat on me as well?" He'd kill any man within the club who even thought of turning against the Straight to Hell MC. This was a blood loyalty, live or die. There was no getting out unless you were six feet under.

Simple as fucking that.

"What if we got him to bring in the daughter?" Reaper asked.

"What?"

"The rat's kid. You wanted her. I could call Brick off, and this guy could bring her straight to us. We take care of both problems then."

"Yes, don't kill me. I'm sorry. It was all Richard's idea. He said we could do it if I followed his orders."

Lord kicked him away. "You think I want to hear what a weak-ass piece of shit you are? It doesn't surprise me you'd rather save your own ass by luring a woman here."

He stepped back.

His need for blood was strong, but he couldn't have the daughter out there running her mouth off. He didn't know the full extent of Richard's relationship with his kid. They may not be on speaking terms, but that didn't mean they didn't talk on the phone, and club business was at stake. He wasn't going to take any risks.

"You've got one week. Bring me Richard's kid, and I'll see how generous I am as to whether I let you walk away." He wouldn't. The only reason he was going to use this bastard was for a means to an end. This entire shitshow needed to be cleaned up. With a cop locating the daughter, he didn't have to deal with potential damage control when it came to bringing her here.

All this had done was make his life easier and prolonged the cop's until she arrived.

Then he'd get to have his blood.

****

"Law?" Becky asked.

"Yes, law. As in becoming a lawyer. You know,

protecting the innocent and sending rotting assholes to jail?" Ally said.

"I know what law and becoming a lawyer is all about, but isn't that, like, really hard?"

Ally couldn't help but laugh, putting down a shot glass before turning away to deal with another customer. She loved her job and Riches Bar, and the tips paid well. The hours were crazy, but she was able to afford rent and even consider going to law school. Of course, if she did actually decide to go through with her plan, she was going to be so fucking broke. The thought of the debt alone was enough to make her cry.

She never did.

At nineteen years old, she'd been working for a long time. Ever since she was fifteen, she'd held a job. During high school, part-time at a diner. Through the summer, she worked two jobs, and since she turned eighteen, she'd been working at Riches Bar in the evening and overnight, and she still worked at the diner for lunch. She loved to work. It meant earning legal money, being able to pay her bills, and not having to depend on her father.

Not that she ever could.

Her father was a bad seed and got mixed into way too much sketchy business. Getting away from him was the best thing she'd ever done. He sent her birthday and Christmas cards on occasion, and he tried to talk to her during New Year's, but she wasn't interested in building up a relationship with him at this point. All the motions were only skin deep—he didn't really care about her.

No, the time he'd considered selling her to pay for a debt, that had been the final straw. He'd never actually done it, but it had gotten so close that she'd feared for her life. Unlike Becky, she didn't come from a great family or have a wonderful childhood.

When her mother left her trapped in a closet, it had taken her father three days to come home. She'd been eight, screaming to be let out.

She pushed those memories aside, and instead, turned back to her friend.

"You don't think I've got it in me?" Ally asked, looking at her friend.

"I believe you have it in you. I've never met anyone as smart or as determined as you, but when it comes to the law, who exactly would you be protecting?"

"The innocent."

"Honey, don't take this the wrong way, but you're not the best judge of character."

"Says who?"

"Me. For one thing, you've got the whole issue with your dad. Do you really think you can make unbiased opinions?"

"It was an idea."

"Last week you wanted to be a surgeon. Do you remember?" Becky asked.

"Why are we having this discussion?"

"You were the one who came to me. Let's see, in the last three months, you've wanted to become a nanny, a forensic scientist, an analyst, a physiotherapist, an owner of some app or another."

"Okay, I get it."

"I'm not done. In the past week, we've gone from surgeon, beautician, lawyer, hairdresser, designer, and I think one of my favorites was quilting as well."

Okay, she was fickle. Or maybe she was just lost with nothing and no one to ground her. Ally didn't know what she wanted or needed out of life.

She rolled her eyes. "You make it sound like I have no direction."

"Honey, you don't."

"So, I'm undecided about how I want to take my future." She shrugged.

"Have you ever thought about maybe applying for another job and seeing where that takes you?"

"Of course, I have, but I don't want to let Ben down." Ben was the owner of Riches place, and he'd given her a chance even though she'd never been a barmaid. Even though she got the job with a fake ID and he knew it. "It feels a little like I'm not being loyal."

"Please, you are loyal, but he'll understand that even you want to have a life and do something else. Not everyone stays in the same job forever. I don't know why we're having this discussion. You're nineteen. We should be fucking our problems away until Monday morning."

"Yeah, you can do that and not worry about the giant headache you're going to get, and with work."

Becky didn't work. She didn't need to work. She was rich and her parents supported her. Her best friend was also five years older than her, and she'd already done a couple of years in college and hated it.

"Sweetheart, you know I'd hire you in an instant."

"I know, but that doesn't feel right. You're my friend." She put her hand over Becky's. "I'll figure out something else. I don't know what came over me. I woke up really restless. Like I need to do something or something bad is going to happen. I don't know."

"I think you need to find a good man, one with a nice big dick, and have a little fun. That's what I believe."

"I've got to serve. Are you sticking around for a little bit?"

Becky's cell phone went off. "Ugh, I was going to stay, but it would appear my presence has been

SAM CRESCENT AND STACEY ESPINO

demanded by those of importance."

"Your parents?"

"Yes, my daughterly persona is needed." Becky leaned over the counter and Ally kissed her cheek. "Good night."

"Night."

"And think about what I said," Becky said.

"Sorry, I won't be leaving here tonight with a man."

"Pity. You could have at least done something more interesting. Later."

Ally waved at her friend. The rest of her evening was uneventful. No fighting. Just serving. Beer, shots, whiskey, some cocktails.

Ben came to join her toward the end, to hustle out the last of the customers. With the doors closed, she stuck around, cleaning up. There were a few broken glasses, which she told him about.

"Ben, can I ask you something?" Ally asked.

"Sure."

"Did you ever go to college?"

Ben laughed. "I did. I took business. I never actually passed it though. I was the guy who was always at the parties. Some of the cocktails you serve are my own creations. Why? Are you thinking of going?"

"Sometimes. I'm not really sure what to do with my life." Her parents hadn't exactly been inspirational on her career choices, and she didn't even know what happened to her mom. The last she'd heard, she was living with a junkie downtown.

"Don't overthink everything. Just find out what you like and go with it. It's all anyone can do."

"Says the guy who owns several bars and clubs across the country."

"Again, a degree didn't get me that. Go on, get

out of here. I'll finish cleaning up. Would you like me to walk you home?"

"No, I came by car. I heard it was going to rain tonight. I didn't want to take any chances."

"You want me to walk you out to your car?"

"I'm good." She didn't like accepting help. A strength or a flaw, she wasn't sure. If she got used to Ben being there for her, it would be impossible for her to imagine going to her car without him. She'd been taking care of herself for so long, accepting help was difficult. "See you tomorrow night."

"Night, Ally."

She grabbed her bag and jacket from the back, letting herself out the delivery entrance, toward the back of the parking lot. Her car was beneath a flickering lamp. It hadn't been flickering for days, and now it suddenly decided it wanted to be on the out.

Shaking her head, she moved toward her car, key at the ready. The alarm was shot, and she didn't want to waste any cash, so she pressed the key into the lock just as she was leaned against the front of the car.

"Ally Prixman, you're under arrest."

"Wait, what the hell?"

Her hands were forced behind her back, cuffed, and she was pulled toward a police car. One she recognized as being from her town.

Resisting arrest was against the law, so she complied. If she did nothing wrong, she'd be okay. Did he know she was working at the bar underage?

Panic consumed her.

She didn't know what the hell was happening. All she knew was if a cop was arresting her for nothing, it had to do with her father.

What had he done now?

Chapter Two

Lord sat up in bed. It was fucking two in the morning. The cell phone display lit up in the darkness. He hadn't expected this call so soon.

"Don't tell me there's a problem already." Lord ran a hand through his hair and rolled out his shoulders. He'd been lifting heavy in the gym all afternoon, and his body felt stiff.

"I have her," said Bobby Joe Ranger. The rat cop's voice had a musical edge, like he'd just won the lottery. "She's in the back of my cruiser as we speak."

He twirled a bullet on his nightside table, pleased the plan had come together so smoothly. It seemed too good to be true.

"You have Richard's daughter? Ally Prixman?"

"Yes, Lord. I have her, just like I said I would."

"You woke me from bed, you better not be bullshitting me," said Lord.

"I swear it's her. I have her ID and everything."

He exhaled, looking at the clock again. "I'm not getting out of bed. Lock her in your trunk for the night. I'll meet back at your place first thing in the morning."

"Whatever you want. I'll be ready."

Lord turned off his phone and tossed it on the empty side of his bed. It would be hard to fall back asleep now. His mind was a blur of Richard's betrayal, the lies, the deception. He'd trusted the bastard, given him a job, and he got nothing in return but grief. Lord valued loyalty above all else. He'd give his life for any man in his club. Knowing Richard was trying to sell off his secrets, even using one of the cops on his payroll to make it happen, was like a knife to the back.

Now he had the man's daughter.

Using family members against his enemies had

always been the best revenge. It was better when they watched, so they could feel the same pain they caused for the club. With Richard six feet under, Lord would still get satisfaction knowing the rat's only heir would join him, ridding the world of his bloodline. He'd toy with her a bit, make her suffer, remind her what a bastard her father was when he'd been breathing. Then he'd put a bullet in her head.

He could already feel the sense of closure. The unique satisfaction that came with revenge.

It was time to move on from this betrayal and work on strengthening and expanding the Straight to Hell MC.

When he woke up next, the early morning sun shone right in his face. He rolled to the side to check the time, immediately remembering the call from last night. It was time to clean this shit up.

He opened his bedroom door and whistled. One of the club whores ran up the hall toward him within seconds. Lord grabbed her by the back of the neck and she froze. "Tell Brick, Reaper, and Stump to gear up. We're heading out as soon as I take a shower."

"Want me to join you?"

He looked down at the half naked woman. She wasn't unattractive. He was well aware that getting into his bed was an honor for the club whores, but he had no interest lately. Lord would say he'd lost his fucking libido, but he had no trouble getting his dick hard. It was the dirty pussy he tired of. At forty years old, he wasn't the same man he was in his youth. He wasn't looking for a connection, and only when he was extremely pent-up did he ever allow the whores near his cock. It seemed every year he grew darker, withdrew more, and lost bits of his humanity along the way. Some said he was heartless, others said he lacked a conscience. All the rumors were true.

Lord washed up in the shower, running both hands through his hair and allowing the water to flow down over his muscles. He was sore, but it made him feel alive. After he dealt with the cop and the girl, he'd push himself in the gym again. It was his outlet, gave him focus, and reminded him to keep disciplined in every aspect of his life. His body and his rank were testament to his dedication.

By the time he made his way to the yard, his men were ready to go, geared up, and packing heat. He nodded his approval as he approached his bike. The chrome glistened in the morning light.

"Where we heading, boss?" asked Reaper.

"You wanted the cop to get the girl for us. He got the girl."

Lord lifted his leg and straddled his bike.

He could hear the unspoken words from his enforcer, but the bastard knew better than to open his mouth. Reaper had a soft spot for women. There was no room for weakness in their world. The girl was going to die, regardless of Reaper's opinion. There was no balancing right and wrong, only their unique form of justice. The Straight to Hell MC had a reputation for a reason. It was Lord's job to ensure they weren't seen as weak or ripe for extortion. If his men were more like him, lacking complete empathy for their enemies, they'd be stronger. Their human nature kept bringing down the club.

He revved his engine, glared at his enforcer, then led the way out of the club.

The drive out to the cop's country home was quiet this early. They drove past countless acres of farmland, dotted with the occasional homestead or herd of cattle. He remembered bits and pieces of a broken childhood. The shed out back, the beatings, the bloodied rope. Being reminded he'd never amount to anything.

Lord had spent most of his forty years trying to forget the past.

When he was around twelve, he lost sight in his right eye. His stepfather was to blame. The motherfucker would hurt his mother while he watched, and the day he tried to intervene, he was left scarred and blinded in one eye. His stepfather said not to watch if he didn't like what he saw. The bastard used a metal rake from the barn, pinned him in the corner where they stored the hay, and thrashed him over and over until he lost consciousness.

He'd been skinny and helpless way back then.

Things were different now.

Lord had learned to turn off his emotions. Permanently. It was better that way. He'd become stronger mentally and physically and would die before he became the victim to any man again.

He snapped back to the present when he nearly lost control on the dirt shoulder of the road. Lord refocused and picked up the pace, only a few more miles until his destination. He couldn't let old memories toy with his head. It was easy to slip into oblivion—he knew that all too well. He had to black it out, push the pain, guilt, and shame so far fucking down into the abyss that they couldn't mess with his head.

Bobby's old farm appeared ahead, and Lord slowed down his bike before turning onto the unpaved drive. The other bikes settled around him, cutting their engines on cue.

"She alive?" asked Reaper.

"Don't worry about it. She won't be for long." Lord headed toward the house, but Bobby Joe Ranger came stumbling off the porch, pulling on a plaid shirt as he neared.

"Good morning," said Bobby.

Lord nodded toward the cruiser.

"Oh. Yeah, she's just where you told me to leave her."

It had been a frigid night. Maybe the girl was already dead.

The cop walked along a beaten path, his keys jangling in one hand. He unlocked the trunk and flung it up, a huge smile on his face. "It was so damn easy. I picked her up as soon as she left work last night."

His VP stepped forward first, glancing into the open trunk. There was no sound, no movement.

"Boss, how old you say this chick was supposed to be?"

He narrowed his eyes, looking over at Brick. "Why?"

"She looks young."

Richard Prixman had been older or at least he had some fucking city miles on him. Lord expected a woman in her thirties, but when he joined Brick at the open trunk, those big green eyes staring at him were pure innocence.

He looked over at the cop. "How old is she?"

The cop handed him her license. "Just turned nineteen. Works at a local bar. No record. No location on the mother."

Lord looked at the license, then back at the girl. "Get her out of there."

Brick and Stump unceremoniously dragged her out, dropping her down on the dirt by his feet.

"She's a big bitch. It wasn't easy getting her in there by myself," said Bobby.

Lord froze in place, staring at the cop, suddenly feeling the overwhelming urge to punch the smug look off his face.

"Lord?"

He returned to the present, squeezing and releasing his fist to calm himself down. Stump stood next to the girl, a questioning look on his face.

This was the day he'd been waiting for, so why did it feel all wrong?

Lord walked over to his men and the girl sitting on the dirt, the sound of each booted foot distinct in the early morning hush. He crouched down, his leather jacket creaking as he leaned over his knees. He reached out one arm, using a curled finger to tilt her face toward him.

"What's your name?"

"I told you it's her, Lord. There's no mistaking it," said the cop.

Lord whirled his head to the side. "Did I fucking ask you a question? Keep your mouth shut if you know what's good for you."

He returned his attention to the blonde.

"What's your name?"

She swallowed hard. "Ally."

"Ally what?"

"Ally Prixman."

He nodded. "Then you're exactly the girl we've been looking for. Do you know why you're here?"

She shook her head. "I'm guessing this is because of something my dad did?"

Why was he noticing the bruise forming on her temple or the way her full lower lip quivered? He usually started these interrogations with a lot less conversation and a lot more pain.

"Richard Prixman. You don't look anything like him," Lord said.

She shrugged. "He was a sperm donor, that's

about it."

Lord chuckled, so did Brick.

"Well, regardless of how you two spent the holidays, he's still your blood, and that motherfucker screwed me over."

"What did he do this time?" she asked. "And who are you?"

He smirked, and it wasn't the kind before he gutted a man. It was a real fucking smirk because, for some odd reason, this girl amused him.

Lord stood up, stretching out his legs. He motioned for Stump to get her to her feet.

He paced back and forth.

"Your father tried to sell me out. He abused my trust, and I don't take that lightly." He stopped, running one hand through his hair. "As for who I am, sweetheart, have you heard of the Straight to Hell MC?"

****

Of course, she had. *Oh my God, oh my God, oh my God.*

She knew her father had dealt with a lot of unsavory characters, but nothing like this. Did he not realize what he was doing? You never crossed an MC, especially not one notorious for bloodshed and making people disappear. She'd worked at Riches Bar for a while now and heard a lot of talk. There was no way she was naïve to what the hulk of a man in front of her was capable of.

And Ally didn't need to know this man's rank. Without a doubt, he was the one in charge, the prez of the club. He moved with confidence and restrained power. For a biker, he was ruggedly attractive, even with the grisly scar on the side of his face. Or maybe in spite of it.

She couldn't tell how much of him was covered

in tattoos but she saw ink peek out from under his sleeves and collar. He was huge and hard with muscle. A short beard covered a strong jawline. How could such a delicious-looking man be the one to end her life?

Becky would kill her if she knew how wet Ally was for a dirty biker, one ready to slaughter her for sins she never committed. *Unless*...

"Did he sell me to you?"

He looked taken aback, so she knew she'd be wrong in the assumption. Part of her was actually disappointed. If she had to belong to a man, why not this one? She pushed her twisted thoughts away and focused on her reality. The one where bikers treated women like trash, cheated on them, and beat them without a second thought. She didn't want to be a man's punching bag.

"Now there's a thought," he said. A devilish little smile revealed the crinkles next to his eyes. Why did it have to turn her on? Had she ever seen eyes so black?

She kept quiet.

"When's the last time you saw your father?"

Ally shrugged. "I can't even remember it's been so long. Last time I saw him, he wanted to borrow two hundred dollars for a debt."

"Did you give it to him?"

She scoffed. "I have ten cents in my bank account."

The man chewed on his lower lip as if conflicted. She hadn't moved, even though her entire body ached. Then he stepped away and talked to one of the other bikers wearing cuts.

"Sure thing, Lord." Then the biker grabbed the cop from last night by the sleeve and led him away toward the barn behind them.

Her nerves began to pick up. She was next. They were both dead.

Ally attempted to think of anything to distract him from killing her, to appeal to any shred of humanity left inside of him.

"Why do they call you Lord? Is your club like a cult or something?"

She immediately regretted her words, holding her breath and tensing.

He raised an eyebrow. "It's just a name. Don't read so much into everything."

The guy holding her exhaled a frustrated sigh, giving her a jostle. "What are we doing with her, boss?"

"Relax."

The way he looked at her was unnerving or titillating, she wasn't sure. He reminded her of a wolf sizing up its prey. She shouldn't be in this situation to start with.

"How much does my father owe you? Why aren't you after him instead of me?"

It wasn't like she'd be able to pay off his debt for him, but it still wasn't fair for her to have to pay for his sins. She'd never done anything wrong. Ally even released spiders rather than killing them.

"Your father's already dead."

Her mouth parted, but no words came out. She hated her bastard father, but knowing he was dead shocked her to the core. And made her more aware of her dire circumstance.

"The Straight to Hell MC is known for a lot of things, I'm sure, but one thing in particular. Care to guess?"

She shook her head.

"Revenge. When we deal with a rat, they're not the only one to suffer. Torturing and killing their loved ones sends a strong message to any other fucker thinking to do the same thing. Wouldn't you agree? It's worked very well for us."

Her eyes began to fill with tears. She held her breath and tried her best not to let her emotions spill over. There were so many dreams she had that would be left unfulfilled. No one would miss her.

A loud gunshot echoed from the barn and she gasped, instinctually rushing forward, clinging to Lord's t-shirt. The guy beside her attempted to pull her back, but Lord stopped him.

She let her hands slowly fall away from him, and she stared down at the ground, never feeling so alone. The third biker rejoined them. The cop had to be dead. Dead like her father. Dead like she'd be soon.

"I'm sorry," she whispered.

He ran both his hands into her hair at the sides of her head, forcing her to look at him. He exhaled in a near growl. An angry sound.

"You're your father's daughter. All I've thought about the past few days is wiping your bloodline off the face of the earth—to see you broken and bloodied, begging for me to end your life, only to keep prolonging your suffering. I imagined that fucking Prixman watching from heaven or hell or wherever the fuck he is."

Tears fell down her cheeks, pooling where his hands met her cheeks. "He wouldn't care."

"It's better when they care. Makes the torture more satisfying."

She let out a soft, shuddering breath.

"Who do you live with?" he asked.

"Myself. I've been alone a long time."

"Kids?"

She frowned. "I'm only nineteen."

"I know girls on their third kid by your age," said Lord. "Nothing surprises me."

"I'm a virgin."

Why did she feel the need to blurt out that fact? His jaw tensed, a look of pure evil passing over his vision. Her knees felt weak, but she forced herself to keep it together.

He stared at her for the longest time. Then he released his hold on her head and led her to where the four Harleys were parked. "Burn the cruiser. Burn the barn."

"Yes, Lord," said one of the men.

"This is over. Meet me back at the club when this shit is cleaned up."

He mounted his bike, then revved the engine. Lord drove off and she immediately tensed up, not wanting to be alone with the other three bikers. Were they going to burn her alive? Did they do all the horrific dirty work for him?

Before she had a full-blown panic attack, he circled around over and over until the dirt and grass created a halo around where she stood. He stopped dead in front of her, supporting the bike with his booted foot. Lord nodded behind him.

She was so confused.

"Not too bright, are you? Get on the fucking bike."

Ally had never been on a motorcycle, and as she squeezed on behind his massive frame, she realized she'd never been this close to any man. When he hit the gas, she quickly wrapped her arms around his waist, holding on for dear life. He pressed one hand to hers for a few moments. His skin was warm and rough. The protective gesture seemed uncalled for when he had her fate mapped out.

Within minutes, they were gone. Away from the farm, away from the other bikers, away from what she thought would be her final resting place.

Now it was the future that worried her.

Where was he taking her? Why was she still breathing?

All she could do now was rest her head against his back, hold on, and watch the world flash by.

Chapter Three

Taking her hadn't been part of the plan, but the one thing Lord was used to was adapting. He knew in his gut killing her wouldn't bring him any kind of pleasure. Her grip tightened around him and he liked it. He could never tolerate touch—until now. He savored the feel of those thick, juicy thighs holding on to him. It had been a long time since he'd seen a curvy woman like her.

The current women of the club were slender. Some were nothing more than skin and bone. Just feeling this woman, he knew she was different. It was a gut feeling that had taken him by surprise as soon as he laid eyes on her. There was no denying it.

His cock hardened at the thought of seeing her naked. He didn't know what the fuck to do with her.

When her head rested against his shoulder, he tensed up. He hated being touched, but this … her touch didn't piss him off. Was she trying to get comfort from him? This chick confused him, no doubt about it. There was no way any woman should ever want to get any kind of anything from him. He was a monster, through and through. He'd learned by pain and suffering himself to never let anyone in.

Ally.

That was her name.

Lord wanted to know more. Every detail. Was Ally short for Allyson, Alysia, something else? For some fucked-up reason, he actually cared to find out.

He also needed to constantly remind himself that she was the enemy. The daughter of a rat bastard. They weren't friends.

Gritting his teeth, he tried not to think about what he really wanted. The moment she'd asked if her father had sold her to him, he'd seen the glint in her eyes. Even as her body had shaken in fear, he knew she was attracted to him, and what was more, she hated herself for it as well.

Ally needed to learn to keep her mouth shut because she'd given him a wicked idea. Pressing his foot to the gas, he rode all the way back to his clubhouse, which was in the middle of nowhere. Not a single house in sight, which was exactly how he liked it.

He hated most people and learned at an early age that the world was made up of liars and cheats. He'd simply become the master, and their fates were now in his hands. There were no squeaky-clean people within his world. They were all after something from him, and like always, he had a price.

Not once did he stop on his journey back home.

Bobby's death didn't bother him. Tying up loose ends was all part of the deal, and Bobby had fucked up big time. He had no doubt that the only reason the cop went out to find this girl was because he was hiding something himself.

People lied.

The words were a constant mantra in his head.

They lied and cheated.

The gates to the clubhouse were already open. Several club whores were huddled together in a corner. They hadn't even bothered to grab a jacket to ward off the cold. Mini skirts and revealing tops in case one of the brothers looked their way.

He cut the engine. "Get off," he said.

Ally let him go and he wasn't surprised when she ended up a heap on the ground, to which the women in the corner laughed.

"Get lost before I kick your asses out," he said, yelling so they knew he wasn't kidding around. Again, he didn't know why their laughter bothered him. Ally stood up, red-faced, and stared at the ground.

"I've never been on a bike before. It was a new experience."

He should have warned her. She'd heard the cop get killed, not to mention the fact she'd been taken against her will, and well, to normal people, it made for a really hard day.

Lord stared at her for several moments. Her blonde hair was long. He hadn't gotten too close back at Bobby's house, but the locks easily fell to her ass, but it wasn't dull or lank. There were waves, and it looked silky to touch. The jeans and shirt she wore covered up her curves. They weren't exactly flattering clothes, but what he'd felt up close, well, that had gotten him really interested.

This shouldn't be happening to him. He didn't want a woman in his life, or in any part of his world. It pissed him off to even be thinking about keeping her.

A virgin.

He wet his lips. Those were the words she whispered to him. No man had ever touched her. Lord tapped his fingers against his thigh as his men began to arrive. Reaper would have been the one to stay behind to see the end of the job done.

None of the men stopped to greet him as he stared at Ally, who continued to watch everything.

He saw her taking it all in like a damn sponge. She was so young and innocent. He didn't know how Richard had managed to keep a daughter oblivious to the demons of this world. Lord ran a hand down his face, trying to clear the fog from his mind.

There was no denying what he wanted. Even now, his dick made it perfectly clear what he'd be happy to do.

Hating how weak he fucking felt at responding to

a woman, he grabbed her arm none too gently and marched her through the clubhouse, going straight to his office. A couple of women tried to gain his attention, but one look at his face and they were all scampering away. No one wanted to be in the firing line, and he was ready to cause pain and destruction. He kicked his door closed and released Ally with a shove. She fell against his sofa, and he went straight to his liquor cabinet. A whiskey was what he needed.

After pouring himself a large shot, he downed it in one go. His body was becoming old and jaded. It didn't even burn as it slid down anymore. The first time he'd tasted whiskey was when he was fourteen, not long after another beating from his stepfather. He never hit back, at least not that time. No, it had been a couple of weeks later that he'd finally punched the fucker back, and that feeling had given him a giant rush.

He pushed those thoughts aside and instead focused on the sexy-as-fuck blonde in front of him. She sat, her legs closed, hands resting on her thighs. She looked sweet and kind. He didn't want to think about kindness, not right now when he wanted to fuck her.

"Do you want to be mine?" he asked.

She frowned at him. "You said he didn't sell me to you."

"Didn't answer my question."

"You didn't answer mine."

He threw the glass down and charged at her. She shrank back as he put his hands at either side of her head, trapping her against the sofa. There was nowhere for her to escape, and that was exactly what he wanted. Even though she'd been camped out in Bobby's trunk all night, she smelled good.

A virgin.

Lord couldn't recall ever meeting such a woman

in all of his life. The first time he had sex was with a woman in her thirties who was more than willing to teach a sixteen-year-old how to please a woman. He'd learned fast how to get what he wanted from the opposite sex.

With Ally in his life now, he wondered if he could have a little toy all to himself. Would she be willing to give herself to him to keep her life?

She swallowed hard. "You're scaring me."

"Good. I told you I intended to kill you. And look, you're still breathing."

"You think I should be grateful to you for that?"

He loved the fact she had a spine. No woman had spoken to him like this in a really long time. Stroking a finger down her cheek, he expected her to cower away, but little Ally was full of surprises as she didn't respond. She glared at him.

Lord chuckled.

This was the most entertainment he'd experienced in ages. He sat back on the coffee table as he studied her. "I've got a proposition for you."

"What?"

He stared at her for a moment, wondering if he was making the biggest mistake of his life. He wanted to fuck her, sure. Play and toy with her. Push her boundaries and limits, but she was still a woman, and that made him stop. Women were a pain in the ass. They always had an agenda, and he knew women were master manipulators.

Still, his dick wanted attention. The women who passed themselves around the club were no longer welcome to him. He had no desire to even go near them.

"How much do you value your life?" he asked.

"Is this a trick question?"

He got up and poured himself another generous shot of whiskey, and he decided to give her one as well.

Picking up the small glass, he moved back toward her.

She grimaced. "I don't drink."

"Bobby picked you up outside of a bar. Don't fucking lie to me. A virgin you may be, but you drink."

She stared at the glass then took it. "I work there, but that doesn't mean I drink hard liquor." She leaned forward and placed the full glass on the table. Her hands went back to her thighs.

He noted her shaking and continued to stand, watching her every move.

"What do you want from me?"

"I wanted you dead."

"Why? You don't know me." She sighed. "I get it. You hated my dead-beat dad and he owed you money and all that, but I'm not him. Do you expect to pay for your father's sins?"

"I did." He pointed at his eye and her face paled. She didn't need to know that he got the scars from his stepfather. If his own father hadn't fucked off when his mother was pregnant, maybe things would have gone differently. Maybe not.

"Oh, I'm so sorry." Her voice had faded to a whisper. It was the sweetest fucking sound he'd ever heard.

"Cut the crap. Just tell me what you'd be willing to do to live?"

****

She was going to wake up.

Ally kept on pinching her thigh, hoping the bad dream that felt very, very fucking real would fade and she'd go back to being normal again. Maybe she'd passed out in the cold and was in a hospital bed right now.

The sharp bursts of pain weren't helping.

She gritted her teeth.

"Answer me!" His growl cut through her prayers and she stood up for the first time.

Her heart raced, and she felt a little sick from how scary he was acting. She wanted to slap him, but instead, with her hands clenched, she frowned at him. "I don't want to die. I don't think it's right that you would dare to expect me to pay because my dad is an asshole. I already got the memo on how bad he is, was, and I know you've killed him. So what? You did me a favor."

Shut up, Ally. This is why you always get into trouble. Why you've lost several jobs. She struggled to get her emotions into check. It was embarrassing, and right now, it wasn't exactly helping her cause.

Lord reached out and grabbed her around the neck with one hand. He pinned her up against the wall. For a few seconds, she thought he was going to choke her, but he didn't hold her tightly enough. There was no reason to even claw at his arms.

"We are all fucking pawns to the sins of our parents. I can't trust you, Ally. You're a liability."

"You made me one. I hadn't spoken to him in months, if not years. He hated me." She gripped his wrist, hoping in some way she'd be able to stop him from killing her. It was laughable for her to even believe she could try to stop a powerhouse like him.

He was bigger, stronger, harder. She didn't hurt anyone or anything, while Lord killed without remorse. His reputation preceded him.

"You're starting to irritate me," he said.

"And you're not exactly my favorite person. Actually, you're an asshole, too." She pursed her lips together, expecting him to choke her to death, only, he smiled.

He pressed his entire body against her.

His cock.

Oh, my. She felt it flush to her stomach and she tensed up. Her was pussy soaked through. How was it possible to be aroused by this man when she hated him with every single fiber of her being? He was horrible, an unforgiving bully. Yet, here she was, her virgin body betraying her.

She hoped he wouldn't notice.

Lord smirked. "I bet you're soaking wet for me right now."

"I don't know what you're talking about."

"No?" The hand on her throat moved, and before she realized what was happening, his hand was inside her pants, touching her bare pussy. The jeans she wore were loose, as were her panties. She'd lost some weight due to the fact she couldn't afford much food, and she didn't have the funds to buy new clothes either.

There was a time her clothes had been too tight.

Not anymore.

She closed her eyes, mortified as he felt how wet she was. His dominance aroused her even more, when it should have sickened her. She'd never bowed down to a man, not even her father. She wasn't a pushover, and yet here she was with a total stranger threatening her life, and she was panting for more.

This wasn't her. Or was it?

"So, my little virgin, you think this is you not being wet?" He chuckled as he rubbed his nose against her cheek, going around to her neck and biting down on her pulse. The sharp bite of his teeth felt so good. "I bet I could have you riding my dick like a good little slut."

She moaned.

Damn him.

"You're not saying stop."

She wanted to. Her lips opened to scream the word, but he did something magical over her clit. She'd touched herself many times, but she hadn't been able to make it feel this good. What was he doing to her? This was better than anything she'd ever experienced.

All of a sudden, the pleasure was gone.

Ally opened her eyes and her mouth parted as he put his fingers to his own and licked her right off him.

"You know, Ally, I've got a proposition for you."

She couldn't even think, and he wanted to negotiate. She didn't have the first clue how to react right now. All she wanted to do was take his hand and shove it right back into her panties, but that wasn't right. She wasn't a whore.

"What do you want?" she asked.

Where she was able to find the words was beyond her. Talking wasn't exactly in her wheelhouse right now. He took her hand and moved her back toward the sofa.

She let out a little gasp as his door was suddenly rattled and shouting could be heard from beyond, but no one came in.

He picked up her glass of whiskey and swallowed it down. He'd taken three shots and still looked normal. No signs of him appearing tipsy or the alcohol going to his head. Working in a bar, she'd watched men turn nasty from drinking.

"Do you want to live?" he asked.

"You know I do." She had so much to live for. It was corny, but she wanted the four kids, a husband, a beautiful home, many dogs and cats, rabbits as well. Living with nothing and no one, she wanted it all.

Dying because of her father wasn't an option, not for her. He hadn't been worth the time to even mourn. She knew it made her a bad person to think that, but she was more than glad he was dead.

The smile he gave her didn't exactly make her feel safe or happy.

"I'll allow you to live, but in return..." He stopped and kept on looking at her. Ally didn't interrupt. She knew whatever he was thinking couldn't be good. Nibbling on her bottom lip, she waited. Her nerves picked up with every passing second. "Your body is mine to do with as I please."

She wasn't expecting that. "Excuse me?"

"I want you to be my fuck toy."

Silence rang out.

A fuck toy?

Ally couldn't believe she'd heard him right, but with the way he looked at her, there was no mistaking his meaning. He knew what he wanted.

Avoiding his gaze, she stared down at her hands. She'd been pressing her nails into the flesh of her thighs. The sharp bite of pain made her stop.

"You ... you, want to have sex with me?" she asked. She didn't dare look up.

Sex.

He reached out, his finger going to her chin. He tilted her head back so she had no choice but to look at him. He didn't allow her to take an inch.

"Yes. What I want, Ally, is for you to be mine. Your tits, ass, and pussy, they're all mine. You'll be at my beck and call. You won't work. I keep odd hours, so where I go, you'll go. No one else is allowed to touch you. You're going to be mine to use."

She licked her lips.

"Don't make any mistake. I'm not offering you love or a lifetime. When I'm done with you and bored, you can go."

"Just like that?"

"You value your life, so you won't run to the cops."

She wouldn't rat. They'd already killed a cop

right in front of her, so they'd have no problem doing it again or killing her. She wasn't an idiot. Even if he was to let her leave now, she wouldn't even tell her best friend what she'd witnessed. She thought about Becky.

"I have … my friend, Becky. She'll probably be worried about me. We've gotten close the past couple of years. She'd notice if I disappeared."

Lord grabbed his cell phone. "Give me her details."

She nibbled on her lip.

"Ally, I either kill you tonight, or you get to live. Also, if you don't make the right choice, your friend will be on the kill list as well."

She gave him all the details. "You promise you won't hurt her?"

"I don't have a reason to." He clicked his cell phone. "But I can make sure it looks like you just took off. Fickle young girls do it every day."

Ally shook her head. "No, you don't understand. Becky won't believe that."

"For your sake, you better hope she does." He put his cell phone down. "I take it we have a deal?"

She had never belonged to anyone. There was a long list of things she hadn't done in her life. Never dated. Never been kissed. Sloppy gropes from customers didn't count, not even for a second. But sex with this man terrified her. He'd rip her apart, take everything she valued away from her. She'd be like one of the whores lurking around the entrance to the club, and that wasn't who she was.

"I agree, but I have conditions!" She spoke fast, holding her hand up as if in surrender.

"You're a woman. I didn't expect anything less."

He sounded bitter. Already Lord judged her based on the women he'd been with before. Ally was certain he'd never been with anyone like her.

"I can't get pregnant," she said. "I'm not on the pill, so you're going to have to use condoms."

"Not a chance. You think I'm going to give up the opportunity to be inside virgin pussy?"

"You're vulgar, and if you think I'm letting you give me anything—"

"I'm clean, but don't worry, I've got a doctor who can get you the necessary pills." He was on his cell phone again.

"Wait a second, I'm not finished."

"Hurry up," he said, not even looking at her.

"You can't beat me, cut me, or mark me in any way," she said. "I don't like pain."

He looked up, brow raised. "What kind of sicko do you take me for?" he asked. She didn't answer. "Is that it?"

Nothing else came to mind, and she nodded.

What the fuck had she done?

Chapter Four

Lord left the building. Brick was on him within minutes.

"What happened with the girl?"

"She's in my office."

"And?"

"And nothing. I'm keeping her … until I tire of her, anyway."

Brick raised an eyebrow.

"What?"

"It's not exactly your MO."

It was true Lord usually liked things cleaned up quickly. No loose ends. It was completely out of the ordinary for him to keep an enemy of the club around, one he'd planned to torture and kill.

Of course, Brick was taken off guard. He couldn't understand it himself.

"I'm full of surprises today, ain't I? Get one of the girls to bring her food. No one touches her, make sure of it."

"Where you going?"

"The gym."

He didn't plan on changing his schedule for Ally. In fact, he needed to clear his head more than ever right now. He'd made a deal with the devil and wasn't sure if it was the right decision. The things he wanted to do to that virgin body were unholy. But he was heading to the gym instead of dragging her to his bedroom. When had he grown a conscience?

Lord began adding weight to the bar, fitting on the rings one at a time, heavy metal clanging against metal. A couple of brothers were working out in the back, but they kept to themselves. When he lifted, he liked to zone out. He wasn't there for chitchat.

Just before he started his reps, Reaper came rushing into the room.

"We have a problem, Lord," he said. "One of the Skull Nation boys."

"What now?"

"One of our girls from the whorehouse up north was slashed in the face. The fucker told her she could work for them or die."

"Work for them?"

"They're trying to take over the entire town."

Lord shook his head. "Wait a minute." He pointed a finger. "Where was her protection? The whorehouse has at least six brothers keeping watch over the girls."

"I don't have all the details."

The little northern town wasn't of value in itself, but it was waterfront and droves of tourists flocked to the beachfront on a continuous basis. They owned the town, and business was thriving. From sex to drugs, it was a cash cow. Now the Skull Nation MC wanted to move in on their turf, and Lord wouldn't stand for it. His men who'd fucked up and let this unfold would pay. He'd make sure of it. The Straight to Hell MC was supposed to be on top of their game. This never should have happened.

"Where's the girl now?"

"Out front. Gabriel drove her down."

He took one last look at his weights and exhaled his displeasure. Lord slung a hand towel over his shoulder and followed Reaper out of the gym.

Several bikes roared in the yard, Gabriel and the whore from up north the center of attention. Lord walked up to her and grabbed her face by the chin, turning her head from side to side. The knife slash would leave a nasty scar, but she looked otherwise unscathed.

"What's your name?"

"Misty."

"Tell me exactly what happened," he said. "Don't even think about bullshitting me."

"He had a boxcutter. He grabbed me—"

"Was he in the house? Did he pretend to be a customer?"

She sniffled. "No."

"*Where* did this happen?"

"I went for a walk with Amber. We were going for a coffee in town."

Lord ran a hand through his hair. "You tell the boys you were leaving? Or did you just decide it was a good idea to leave yourselves vulnerable?"

She shrugged.

He was about to backhand the bitch but restrained himself. "Who do you work for?"

"You, Lord. I'd never sell out, I swear."

He shifted his attention to Gabriel. "We protect our own. The girls work for us, we keep them safe. That's how this fucking works."

"There was no warning. We're a blip on the map. We never expected something like this to go down."

"No one takes what's ours." He grabbed Misty by the upper arm and shoved her toward Gabriel. "Take Reaper and Stump with you. I want to know exactly what we're dealing with. Report back to me."

If Skull Nation wanted to fuck with him, they'd live to regret it. Depending on how many of them had moved in on the town, he'd make his next move accordingly. His club had run the supply of drugs, guns, and whores along the entire east coast for decades. He may be getting older, but until he was dead and buried, he'd defend everything in their territory.

"What do you want them to do with Misty?"

asked Brick.

"She can still open her legs."

Lord had never raped a woman, and he didn't force them to work for him. His club whores and the many working in his network of brothels were there more than willing and eager to work up the ranks. They loved the money, the attention, and belonging to the Straight to Hell MC. It was one big, fucked-up family. And they all answered to him.

"Boss?"

He turned and glared at Brick. His patience fading quickly. His VP jutted his chin to the far end of the yard. A curvy little blonde was tiptoeing around the buildings, making her way toward the main gates.

For some reason, it didn't push him over the edge like it should. He had to stop himself from smiling. "Bring her to me."

He watched as Brick retrieved Ally and carried her back kicking and screaming over his shoulder. When he set her down on her feet in front of him, he stood with his arms crossed.

She looked up at him with those deceptively innocent eyes. "I was taking a walk."

"That's the best you've got?"

"You never came back to the office. I wasn't sure what you wanted me to do."

"From what I remember, we had a deal. Are you reneging already?"

She shook her head, and it pleased him.

"Want her to ride with me, Lord? I'm heading up north anyway. I can drop her off at the whorehouse and get her out of your hair for good," said Stump.

"This pussy isn't for sale. She belongs to me." He waved a hand in the air, making a circle above him. "Head out. Find out what we're dealing with."

The bikes drove off and onlookers spread out, going back to their own business. Leaving him alone with Ally in the vast, empty yard, the remnants of dust settling.

"You were trying to escape. How far did you think you'd get before I found you?"

"I hadn't planned that much ahead."

He pointed to the armed guards patrolling the entrance. "You wouldn't have made it a foot past the gates. You've already seen what happens to traitors. Now, let's not have this happen again. Understand?"

This time, she nodded. "Who was that other girl? With the cut face?"

He tilted his head to the side. "Who do you think she was? My last conquest?"

"Probably."

Lord narrowed his eyes. She continually tested him, and normally, he'd never tolerate it. There was just something about this particular girl that entertained him.

"She's not my type," said Lord.

He led her back to the clubhouse, walking by her side. Once inside, he told her to take off her sweater.

"What? Why?"

"I own you, Ally. Stop questioning everything and do what I ask."

She looked side to side, her cheeks turning a bright shade of pink. It amazed him how her innocence was such a fucking turn-on. As she unbuttoned the ugly sweater, part of him wanted to soothe her fears. But that wasn't his job. She was just a temporary distraction.

Ally moved teasingly slow.

"Tonight would be good," he prodded.

She slipped it off over her shoulders, revealing a fitted pastel-pink tank top underneath.

"No bra?"

Ally crossed her arms, trying unsuccessfully to hide those big, sloppy tits from him. She scowled. "I know I need one, okay. I always take it off with my uniform before leaving work. It's not comfortable."

"I like you like this. Nothing like a perfect fucking rack."

This time, she made eye contact with him. She definitely wasn't expecting that answer. Little did she know he wanted to drown in those lush curves. His cock was already painfully hard.

"Come closer."

Lord sat on the edge of one of the large wooden bench tables in the main entrance. There were usually a couple of brothers sitting around. Right now, it was just the two of them.

She approached him. Tentatively.

"Closer," he said.

Once she was within arm's length, he hooked his hand around her back and pulled her between his parted legs.

"Lift up your shirt."

She shook her head.

"These are my tits now. You better get used to feeding them to me when I ask."

Ally took a deep breath, not saying another word. Ever so slowly, she pulled up her top until the material stretched over the full sloping peaks. Her nipples were big, ripe buds, making his mouth salivate.

"Give one to me."

He watched as she grabbed her own breast and lifted it toward his mouth, her nipple teasing his lips. When he opened, taking as much of her as he could, she moaned—quickly trying to mask the sound.

Lord suckled her tit, then switched to the other. He was already addicted to Ally. Women with tits half

SAM CRESCENT AND STACEY ESPINO

her size were usually plastic. She was all soft and natural, exactly how a woman should be.

He leaned away, his hand still on her back, keeping her in place. "You liked that."

She didn't answer.

"Cover up. I don't want anyone else seeing this body but me."

Lord wanted to run his hands through her blonde hair. To stare into her eyes. To kiss her. He never kissed women. What was happening to him?

****

Ally had been holding her breath.

This should be a nightmare. She'd had to choose between death or becoming a biker's whore. She chose the latter, and he was already subjecting her to his sexual whims.

Why wasn't she hating this more?

Why did his no-holds-barred sexuality only turn her on?

There was something dark and brutal about Lord that scared her, but also something more, something that pulled her in. She wanted to please him, wanted him to love her. Stupid fairy-tale thoughts wouldn't help her in a motorcycle club, but she couldn't help herself.

She was only nineteen, but she'd been on her own for a long time. It was draining supporting herself while hoping for a better future. Her parents had done a number on her. Lord's possessiveness made her feel wanted for the first time in her life.

But it was all an illusion.

"What's your real name?" he asked.

She raised a brow. "You already know everything about me."

"Ally Prixman. What's Ally short for?"

"Nothing."

"Nothing?"

Ally shrugged. "My mother just liked the name, I guess. Trust me, there're no beautiful stories connected with my life." She took a breath. "I'm just Ally."

He raked his gaze down her body. Everywhere he looked seemed to heat up in return. His beard was thick and masculine, and his scars made her curious, but she didn't dare ask questions.

"You sure you're a virgin?"

She nodded.

"We could charge a pretty fucking penny for you in the whorehouse. Clients pay top dollar for virgins. I could even auction you off for a small fortune."

Her entire body tensed up. She didn't want to be bought and sold by filthy men looking for sex. She wanted to be Lord's. For once in her life, she wanted to matter to someone. In fact, she craved it more than air.

"But I'm a greedy bastard." He stood up, towering over her. "Did you eat?"

"Someone brought me food."

"Was it good?"

She shrugged, not wanted to appear rude. Some half-dressed woman with leathery skin had dropped her off a questionable-looking ham sandwich. With her nerves already flared, she couldn't stomach anything.

He made a sound of disapproval and led her up a series of hallways and a set of stairs. The compound was huge. She'd be terrified here if it wasn't for him, and that didn't make any sense.

Near the end of a hallway, he held open a door. She stepped inside what she assumed was his bedroom. There was a king-sized bed, the blankets bunched up on one side. The room smelled like him, a delicious mix of leather and musk.

"You're the first woman who'll be sleeping in

that bed."

She turned to look at him. He wasn't joking.

"Are you a virgin, too, Lord?" She bit her lip to keep from giggling.

"I don't let whores in my bed."

He walked over to a dark wooden dresser. It looked like an antique. He picked up a two-way radio and began reciting a long list of food dishes. She only half paid attention as she was busy exploring his room, taking in as much as possible. Her future was as uncertain as her feelings.

The colors around her were dark: blacks, browns, and some burgundies. His choice of furniture was classic and timeless. It didn't look like what she'd expect a biker's bedroom to look like, but she had no clue what she actually expected.

"I'm having some clothes sent up for you. You'll need to be comfortable while you're here."

She turned to his voice and saw him set the radio down. "How long will that be?"

"I haven't decided yet."

"What does that mean? Do I get to leave once to take my virginity? Or am I your prisoner forever?"

"You're talkative for a girl who should be dead. I've never gone soft when dealing with rats. And that's exactly what's happening here. I'm not sure what to make of it."

He sounded disappointed with himself for keeping her alive, like being human was a weakness. With his reputation, she was a bit surprised herself.

"My father was a rat, not me."

"And what are you, Ally Prixman?"

Her body immediately tensed. There was this sliver of hope that he felt the same odd pull between them. Maybe his conflict was proof that she was more than an average woman to him. Or she was dreaming and her fantasies would come crashing down in a hurry.

"I'm … I'm just a girl trying to survive in life. Trying to find happiness even when it's constantly being stripped away from me."

"So you're a glass-half-full kind of girl." He winked.

He didn't pity her. It was refreshing.

His calm, deep baritone soothed her. He never made eye contact, just continued doing what he'd been doing despite the fact she'd just left herself vulnerable. It was rare for her to share her deep-seated feelings.

Lord tugged off his t-shirt. His shoulders were huge and corded with muscle, his skin covered in intricate ink. She couldn't stop staring. He was a beast of a man.

He rooted in his drawer, then pulled on a white wife-beater. When he turned, she quickly looked to the floor. The shirt hugged his muscles, highlighting those six-pack abs. Her cheeks felt as hot as a cooktop. Did he realize she'd been staring? Maybe drooling?

He chuckled. "Your age is showing."

She cocked her head to the side. "What does that mean?"

"You haven't lost your innocence." Someone knocked on his door, capturing her attention. "I like that." He went to answer it.

She could smell the food almost immediately. Her stomach rumbled in response. The last time she'd eaten was over twenty-four hours ago, and it hadn't been much. Just some leftovers she'd managed at the bar.

"Sweetheart, give me a hand."

It took her a few seconds to realize he was talking to her. She wasn't used to terms of endearment, even if it was normal for him.

Ally walked closer to the door. Three scantily clad women stood in the hall holding trays of food. Lord handed one to her and told her to put it on the bed.

After the door closed tight, she couldn't help but comment, "This looks a lot better than the sandwich they gave me."

"I'm their prez. They make sure to give me the best."

He set his tray next to hers on the bed. It was a feast, a smorgasbord of food she wasn't used to. Everything looked mouthwatering, like a meal fit for a king—or the president of a motorcycle club. Lord flicked on the large screen television.

"Here are some clothes." He tossed a few women's clothes on the mattress near her. "Why don't you get changed, then we can enjoy this food and watch a movie."

Ally was genuinely confused but was too scared to complain and ruin a good thing. Her curiosity got the better of her and she couldn't keep her big mouth shut.

"Why are you being nice to me?"

He froze, obviously taken aback. Time seemed to stand still as he stared at her, his shoulders back and eyes cold. What had she done?

"Don't mistake kindness for weakness, little girl. Trust me, when the time comes, you won't be able to say the same thing."

She swallowed hard but kept pushing. "Why?"

He growled, his jaw twitching. "Just eat the fucking food."

This time, she kept her thoughts to herself. Honestly, she didn't want things to change between them. Right now, she felt calm and safe—even if she was technically his prisoner. It was a big change from her usually hectic and unpredictable life. She had a roof over her head, clothes, food, and a man she was undeniably falling for.

She knew it wasn't healthy. She knew she had issues. And it still didn't change a thing.

But a man like Lord would never be satisfied with a nineteen-year-old nobody. He was surrounded by drop-dead gorgeous women. Women with experience. Women who knew how to please a man. Like he said, she was just a little girl to him.

She had nothing to offer.

Lord settled on the opposite side of the bed, the mattress dipping and jostling the platters. He leaned on one elbow and popped some fresh grapes into his mouth, glancing over at her as she took a bite of her lasagna. It tasted so good that she couldn't help but let out a little moan.

He smirked but kept quiet.

"Do you have a chef working here?"

"A couple," he said.

She wasn't expecting that answer. There was very little she knew about the inner workings of a motorcycle club. What she'd learned had been from patrons at the bar, things she'd overheard when they got too loud. Other than that, everything was new to her.

After eating her fill, she picked at a few of the sweets. They looked like they were taken straight from the display case of a bakery.

"I haven't eaten this good … ever," she said.

"You're joking."

She shook her head. "I'm not." Ally wiped her mouth with a napkin and plopped back on the oversized pillow.

"Things are going to change. You'll never go hungry again. Your bastard father didn't deserve a daughter like you."

Ally twisted to the side to face him. God, he was sexy as fuck. "You talk like I'm something special. I'm not."

"You're a lot more than you think."

She bit her lower lip, knowing she was about to throw his words back in his face. "I'm a fuck toy, remember?"

"Nothing wrong with that. You're mine. That means only I'm allowed to play. The brothers have the club whores, but they'll never have you."

"And you're the prez. You get anyone you want."

He never refuted. All he did was stare, unnerving her, like he could read her innermost thoughts. Maybe more.

"I guess it's true about green eyes."

Chapter Five

Lord never slept next to a woman. He'd used them for years. They weren't worth getting to know. More often than not, they were a complete waste of time other than having a pussy, ass, and mouth. Staring at Ally, he had to wonder when he'd lost his fucking mind.

Twenty-four hours she'd been in his life and already, she was curled up against him like a kitten. He'd put on a horror movie last night. She wasn't into it at all and spent most of her time hiding behind her hands. It had been cute, watching her. All his life, he'd never met anyone like her.

Sliding out of the bed, he moved toward his en-suite shower. His cock was rock hard after being next to her all night long. That soft, supple body ready for the taking.

Turning the water to cold, he allowed the spray to wash down his body to rinse off the night and fog of the morning. He had shit to do, and sticking around watching Ally wasn't part of his plan.

He needed to get an update on the whore and the Skull Nation MC and to see what he had to do to deal with it. He didn't like anyone attempting to take his turf. The whore could have been lying about how she got that fucking slash. He'd learned a long time ago never to take anything at face value.

Lord touched his own face, wondering what Ally thought of his scars. She didn't stare at him like some people did. In fact, he'd noticed she rarely looked at him at all. Her gaze was either past his shoulder or on his chest. The few times he did catch her looking at him, she'd quickly avert her gaze.

After finishing in the shower, he wrapped a towel around his waist and entered the bedroom to find Ally sitting up in bed.

"Morning," she said.

"Shower is free. There's a clean toothbrush underneath the sink. I'll have some clothes ready for you on the bed."

"I have my own clothes back at my place," she said.

He walked over to her and she shrank back as he put his hands on either side of her body, trapping her in. "Does it look like I give a fuck about what you've got in your old life, Ally?"

"You … you don't have to worry about me or clothes. That's all I meant. I've got plenty back home."

A new insecurity crept up on Lord. He was getting too attached to this girl. The thought of losing her or her wanting her old life unnerved him. He was back in his childhood, hoping for love and compassion but knowing he'd only get pain and rejection. Wanting something he'd never get would only make him weak. Women were fickle and letting down his guard would be one big fucking mistake.

Ally was only riding this out so she could live and return to her old life.

Shaking his head, he stood. "Go shower. I'll tell you what you can and cannot wear." He turned his back on her, going to his closet. Grabbing a pair of jeans and a shirt, he began to get dressed. Ally hadn't returned by the time he was ready. He checked the time, and still nothing. He wasn't a patient man.

He stormed to the bathroom about to bark orders at her, but when he got to the threshold, he stopped. Ally couldn't know he was close, and as he listened, he heard her sobbing. These were not weak tears nor an attempt to try to gain attention. The shower cover hid her from view, but he saw the shadow of her crouched down in the bottom. Her hands over her mouth as she tried to muffle the sound.

Emotions were not something he liked to meddle with.

For several minutes, he listened. She hated him. Hated everything about their arrangements. He was a fool to think there could ever be more.

Stepping back from the bathroom, he licked his lips and yelled, "How long are you going to fucking be?"

Another few seconds' pause. "A couple of minutes. I'll be out soon. I promise." Her voice gave away the fact she'd been crying.

"I'm heading down. I'll have someone come and deal with you."

"Okay."

He wanted her to tell him why she was crying, even if he didn't want the answers. Instead, he turned on his heel and left the bedroom.

On his way down, he found the nearest whore, grabbing her arm and forcing her to face him. "Take up some decent food to my bedroom and get her some clothes as well. Don't fucking test me." He let her go and she stumbled on her heels.

They were way too fucking high to be walking around in the club, but the brothers, for some odd reason, couldn't get enough of the women in high heels. They were completely unsuitable.

Fuck, he was getting old.

He headed into his office and glanced over his cell phone. There hadn't been any missed calls. Collapsing in his office chair, he ran a hand down his face. He hadn't slept that good in such a long time. It just felt … right having her next to him.

His office door opened and he wasn't surprised to see another club whore holding a tray.

"Hi, Lord," she said.

She was already heavily made up. The skirt she wore only just covered her ass and the top, well, there was no point to her even wearing it as he saw nipple. She bent forward, putting his breakfast and coffee in front of him.

When she lifted up, with her head tilted to the side, she nibbled on her lip. "Is there anything else I can do for you?"

"No, get out."

"Oh, well, I'm available to you."

He sat back and looked at her. "Who put you up to this?"

"No one."

Lord picked up his coffee cup and threw it across the room. Hot coffee splashed across all the tiles. "Do I look like the kind of man who likes to be *lied* to!" He growled the word out.

"Tank and Rubber said you needed me. That you wanted a good time. I've been well tested and the brothers are all satisfied. I promise." She offered him a smile and he shook his head.

"Get the fuck out."

He had no desire for pussy that had seen several of his brothers pounding it. The club whores were fun, but he wasn't interested. Not now. Not when he had a precious peach upstairs, ripe for the plucking.

"And tell someone to clean up this fucking mess," he called out after her.

With a knife and fork in hand, he dug into his breakfast, ignoring the next person who came in to scrub at his floors.

His thoughts returned to Ally upstairs. Had they gotten her some good food? What was she thinking this morning? Why did she fucking cry? None of his questions were going to be answered unless he actually asked them, and there was no way in hell he was doing that.

Just as he was about to snap and break something, his cell phone went off.

He checked. It was Stump.

"Tell me what you've got," he said.

"There was an attack on one of the brothels. Guess which one."

"The same one Misty was working at?" he asked.

"You got it. I'm in the security room with Brick. We're checking over the footage. I think Misty is fucking lying. The Skull Nation just walked right in. Five guys. They weren't wearing cuts, but I've seen their ugly fucking faces to know them when I see them. Nothing happened like Misty said," he said. "We've got three dead girls here now, boss. Two men are down, and we've got one customer dead as well. He wasn't a big client."

"I don't give a fuck about the prick. This is still bad for business. No one wants to go to a whorehouse where they could get killed. Find out if the man has any family. Take care of it. Same as the girls."

"Already done. One of the girls has two kids, but they live with the dad. I'll pay him a visit and see what happens."

"And where's Misty now?" he asked.

"She's nicely bound and scared. You'd love her crocodile tears." At the mention of Misty's tears, it made him think of Ally. Misty's tears were understandable. She was going to die, no matter what. Her death was inevitable. Why was Ally crying? Her life was probably fucking miserable. She'd been dealing with her father for years, no matter her age. She had a shit life, he got it. Why did she want to go back to it so badly?

"Get me everything you can. Bring Misty back

here to the club. I think it's going to be another good reminder for everyone of what happens to traitors."

Hanging up his cell phone, he had no doubt in his mind that Misty had been bullshitting him. He had a good sense about people. She'd been the one to tell him she wasn't a rat and how loyal she was. In his experience, someone who said that shit first up was usually a fucking liar.

He had a bad feeling twisting his gut when it came to Ally. Not because she'd done anything wrong, but because she was telling him the truth.

Misty was all lies.

Ally was all truths.

He'd gotten used to people fucking with him. People like Ally were an entirely new experience for him. She confused him on so many levels.

Lord finished his breakfast, sitting back, feeling content, but he still needed a fresh coffee.

He got to his feet and stepped out of his office. The sight just ahead froze him cold.

A couple of the brothers were laughing their fucking heads off as Ally was shoved to the ground and one of the club whores kicked her in the ribs. Ally cried out.

What the fuck was happening?

He also saw how Ally was dressed—a mini skirt and a bikini top that hid next to nothing. And a pair of those ridiculous heels the whores wore. This wasn't what he wanted, and whoever did this was going to fucking pay.

Lord had never lost his shit unless dealing with rats and traitors, but right now, his men and whores had turned him into a liar. He'd told Ally she belonged to him and wouldn't be harmed, and yet here she was. Their deal included her safety.

When one of the women slammed her foot on Ally's hand, the scream that tore through the air cut through him.

Rage flooded his body and he charged to the scene. There was going to be destruction.

****

Pain was all Ally could feel. Never-ending agony. Whoever had stomped on her hand must have broken it.

Her chest hurt, as did her face. One of her eyes had already started to close from the swollen flesh.

Just as she was about to give up, the abuse ceased, and she heard a horrible sound that made her cringe.

Glancing up, she was shocked to see Lord standing there. The look on his face was pure evil.

He'd humiliated her. Nothing she'd felt for him had been reciprocated.

The woman who'd brought her some clothes had told her she was going to have to earn her keep. Rats didn't get a free ride. The skimpy clothes were bad enough, but as soon as they'd pulled her out of the room, the men had mocked her fat ass and horrible tits.

If this was Lord's idea of belonging to him, it sucked. This reminded her of being back in high school—only worse. She never dressed like this and now she was so utterly humiliated. And never so alone.

Death would be preferable about now.

He bent down toward her and she tried to scramble away. When she did, she whimpered as pain exploded from her ankle and wrist. She stopped and stayed perfectly still, panting as he glared. How much more could she endure?

"Ally, don't."

Tears traced down her cheeks.

"Look around you," he said.

She frowned. He wasn't going anywhere, so she tentatively glanced around her. The men who'd been laughing were no longer smiling. In fact, their faces were averted. The women who'd gathered around her and started to hurt her, they were on the ground. One appeared unconscious. She knew without a doubt Lord had put them there.

Staring at him, she felt sick. "I think I'm going to throw up." She tried to stop it but then she leaned over and threw up the food she'd eaten last night, some of it going on Lord's boot.

She sniffled and pressed her hands to her face, trying to compose herself, but it was impossible to do so. Nothing could be worse than this.

Pain.

She hated it. Memories, dark, horrible memories swirled within her mind.

Lord's hand went to her knees and the other went to her back. She wanted to fight him, but she didn't have the energy. This was the last time she'd trust anyone ever again. He lifted her without effort and she wrapped her arms around his neck, holding on to him, hoping he wouldn't drop her.

"I've got you."

She pressed her face against his shoulder, trying not to lose it. She was so close to losing it. That very morning, she'd been sobbing in the shower. Lord was like an entirely different person. One moment hot, the next cold. She didn't know what to think anymore.

Last night, he'd been laughing, joking, making fun of her while she watched that horror film. She hadn't had a carefree night like that in ages. Then this morning, she'd gotten whiplash from the change in him. It wasn't something new for her, but she just hoped Lord was different. Her father had been a classic example, as her mother had been. The drugs and gambling were a perfect reason for them to be constantly up and down.

She couldn't stand it, and this morning, it made her feel like a child. Ally wanted off the rollercoaster.

Lord didn't take her to his bedroom. This time, they entered his office and he gently put her down on the sofa. It was nice and soft. With her good hand, she tried to pull the base of the skirt down, but it was way too small. The woman had also said she wasn't allowed to wear underwear. Could there be anything more humiliating now? Those men had seen her personals.

She'd gone down with a thump to the floor. She'd never been a violent person. All her life, she'd learned to take the punches, the nasty words, the pushing, shoving, all of it. She thought could take it.

Lord stood close and he removed his shirt, exposing his very scarred, but muscular body. She pulled away as he tried to put it on her. She wanted to cover her body, to help soothe the pain, but all those cruel words had hurt her more than the punches.

"Baby, I'm trying to help you."

"I ... it hurts," she said.

He glared and she tried to get the sofa to completely swallow her up. Lord captured her face and held her still. "I didn't order this. I want you to know that."

She didn't believe him. He was the leader.

"Ally."

"My hand hurts. I think it's broken."

She lifted it up for him to see. His gaze didn't waver from hers but she didn't stop holding her hand up for him to see. She could barely move her fingers, and in the short space of time since they'd stomped on it, it was already swelling up.

Lord eventually looked at her hand, but she

watched him as he looked down her arm. Last night, he'd been more interested in sucking her tits than paying attention to her arms.

"These are scars," he said with a frown.

The tip of one finger traced over the old scars.

"*You* have scars."

"What caused these?" he asked.

"A window," she said. "My parents … they'd forgotten about me. They had gone to a party one Friday, leaving me in the car. They'd locked me in, but for two days, no one passed. It was like the car was crushing me. I had to do something. I managed to break the glass, clawing my way out of the front windscreen."

Social services had gotten involved at the time, but they never took her from her parents. After the hospital, she'd gone right back home. Since that experience, small, confined spaces affected her. Being in that police officer's trunk had shaken her up, bringing back old, unwanted memories.

"I'm going to call the doctor." Lord stood, and she stayed seated on his sofa. His shirt was on the cushion beside her. Picking it up, she started to get into it, wanting the comfort of modesty.

She should hate his scent. Lord wasn't going to protect her.

The whores hated her, but they were part of the club.

Pain shot through her body. Sinking her teeth into her bottom lip, she contained any noise as she finally got the shirt over her head. She was so going to suffer for this.

Lord hung up his cell phone and came back to her. When his hands touched her knees, she jumped, jolting her whole body.

A string of curses rushed past his lips and she

tensed up—that didn't help her either. The pain was unrelenting.

Lord stood and left the office.

Being alone here didn't make her feel comfortable. Fear traveled up her spine and she glanced toward the window. If he had guards on the wall, would they kill her if she made it past the wall? A quick death would surely be much preferred than taking constant beatings. After leaving school, she honestly thought she would be free of having to take a punch. She was so stupid.

Lord's door slammed open, making her jump, but what surprised her was the woman behind him. It was the one who'd started this whole thing. She wasn't coming willingly. Lord had her by the hair, dragging her forcibly into the room. He shoved her down on the floor, squatting enough to grab her around the throat.

"You look at this woman right now," he said.

"Please," she whimpered.

"I told you to get her a good breakfast and some clothes. Did I mention anything about hurting her? Humiliating her? You've hurt her hand and ribs, and I can say this, slut, the doctor is on his way. Every single injury she has, I'm going to make sure you're punished with the same. The next time you see my woman, and she *is* mine, I suggest you get on your knees and pray for mercy. Your life is now in her hands. If she wants you dead, that is exactly what you're going to be. Beg for your life!"

"I'm sorry. I'm so sorry."

"Please, stop," Ally said, crying out as she screamed for them to stop. She couldn't handle this chaos.

Pressing a hand to her ribs, she clenched her eyes closed. She counted to ten in her head. Hearing more scuffling, she didn't dare open her eyes.

Lord's hands were back on her knees. "It's okay."

"I don't want you to kill anyone. I can't … don't make me do that. I'm not, I don't want to hurt anyone. Please." She started to sob, hating her own weakness. She should be stronger than this. Weren't shit childhoods supposed to make strong women?

With everything she'd been through, she shouldn't be able to cry.

Lord's head went to hers and she felt his lips against her forehead. She didn't dare open her eyes.

"I won't make you," Lord said.

"When can I go home?" She sniffled. Belonging to Lord no longer made her feel happy. The women here were going to make her life hell. They didn't like that Lord had taken an outsider. They wanted her gone and right now, all she wanted to do was go back to her life. No matter how bad it was.

"Ally?"

She opened her eyes and looked at him. "I don't belong here. I'm not one of you. I … I don't like to feel pain, and I don't want anyone to die because of me. I'm not worth it. Please, just let me go home."

"We had a deal."

"Look at me!" She screamed and cried out at the same time. "I'm ugly. I'm fat and ugly. I've been told it my whole life. I'm not important. If my virginity is what you're after, take it, and let me go, or better yet, kill me. Anything would be better than this. Just please, don't make the pain last. I can't stand it. Please. Please."

Each plea was stronger than the last.

She'd never begged. Not then, but now, with those men, the laughter, she couldn't stand for Lord to see her like that. It was humiliating. To know she would always fail. He needed a woman who was by far better than her.

After a lifetime of always failing, she knew it was time to accept her fate.

Chapter Six

Ally didn't want to order that fucking slut to her death, but Lord didn't have the same conscience. He enjoyed ending her life. Stump was already dealing with the body. And it would be a good damn lesson for anyone else in the club hoping to follow in the bitch's footsteps.

Defy his orders and pay the ultimate price.

Lord splashed cold water onto his face and stared into his vanity mirror.

He never should have taken Ally back to the club.

What had he been thinking?

It was supposed to be simple. Keep a plaything for a couple of weeks, then cut her loose. He was a cold-hearted bastard and never expected a nineteen-year-old girl to tilt his world off its axis. But there was something primal she evoked in him. Something he'd never felt for a woman in his forty years.

Those mixed feelings were toying with him, fucking with his head. He kept trying to fight his urge to protect and claim her, but it was futile. After seeing her broken and half-naked on the ground, there was no more denying how he felt for Ally.

He wanted to protect her. Craved it more than anything. And even though it had only been a couple of days, he wanted to claim her. She was the polar opposite of women he'd fucked with in the past, but she was exactly what he wanted now. Her innocence, sweetness, and even those natural curves were just a few of the qualities pulling him in.

Now, instead of fighting his desire by pushing her away, he'd try to embrace it and make her his woman. It wouldn't be easy. Her trust had been trampled on. But it was a challenge he was willing to take since setting her loose wasn't going to happen.

He felt the presence at the doorway before his VP spoke.

"You okay, boss?"

Lord grabbed a towel and dried his face. "I'm still pissed off."

"I never knew any of that shit was going down," said Brick. "It won't happen again."

He nodded. "You're right. It won't."

Lord left his bathroom, brushing past his VP. The doctor was still with Ally. It gave him the time he needed to clear his head and get some shit sorted out with his wayward club members.

"Stump said everything was handled."

"It wasn't just that whore. Every asshole in this club needs to respect what's mine. I want every brother in church tonight."

"I'll make it happen, Lord."

He paced back and forth, still fuming. The image of Ally injured and crying kept invading his thoughts, making him feel like a failure. Making him want to kill. She'd made him smile last night. Made him feel like a real fucking person and not a broken monster. That was a feat in itself.

Even though she made his cock hard just being in the same room as him, he was content just to watch a movie with her. Why hadn't he claimed what was his? She'd agreed to the deal.

Because he respected her.

Wanted her for more than a plaything even though that was the deal.

She was a good girl, and his own fucking club was destroying her innocence.

"I'm trying to understand," said Brick. "You hated that girl, wanted her dead before you even met her."

"Shit changed."

"Yeah, I get that. But what changed exactly?"

He didn't want his men to think he'd gone soft. And the last thing he wanted was a fucking therapy session. "She's a virgin. It got me to thinking about the future. I'm forty. If I wait forever, I'll never have an heir."

"Okay," said Brick. "So this is about knocking her up?"

"It's not." He grabbed a new shirt out of his drawer and pulled it on over his head. What he needed to do was check up on Ally and the doctor.

"So, she's off-limits?"

Lord stopped dead in his tracks. "You're just getting the idea now? *No one* fucking looks at her."

He was usually on friendly terms with his VP, but not today. His mood was in the shitter and it wasn't going to change until Ally stopped being scared of her own shadow.

There was a lot to deal with at church tonight. Top on his list was ensuring Ally's safety and reminding everyone of his rank in the club. Next was dealing with the Skull Nation bullshit weighing him down. They thought they were smart, probably thought he was cowering as they methodically took over his businesses up north. That was where they were wrong. Lord would make his move and it would be remembered for generations when he did.

As he walked the halls, heading to the infirmary, several brothers and whores tried to kiss ass. They knew what was coming. The devil was pacing in Lord's heart, and that was never a good thing.

He ignored them all.

In the blink of an eye, one girl had taken

precedence in his life. He couldn't believe it himself.

Lord pushed open the door without knocking. Ally was still up on the examination table, a white sheet covering her body. He'd already brought down a full change of clothes before heading up to his room earlier.

"What's the damage?" he asked.

"Nothing's broken," said the doctor, scribbling notes in a file. "But she has some mild ligament damage that will take time to heal. She'll be bruised for a while. The colors are already starting to peek through."

A wave of relief flooded him. He'd do everything in his power and spare no expense making sure she returned to perfect health. "You're certain? You gave her a full exam?"

"I was very thorough, Lord, just as you asked."

He nodded. Ally wouldn't make eye contact with him. Lord wasn't good at coddling or kissing ass, but he knew what he had to do. He'd been an asshole to this girl, and her only sin was being the daughter of a rat.

Richard Prixman was the last thing on his mind. Ally was his problem now. He no longer saw her as an enemy or loose end to wipe out of existence. No, he saw her for what she was—a gorgeous woman he wanted to keep. Not for a week or a month. Forever.

The doctor packed up his travel bag and tipped his hat as he made his way to the door. He'd add the visit to his monthly bill. He was a familiar face around the club. The brothers were always getting themselves into scrapes, and they didn't visit hospitals whenever necessary.

Awkward silence set in immediately once the doctor closed the door behind him.

"I need to get dressed," said Ally, still averting her gaze.

"Okay, so get dressed. I brought you clothes,

remember?"

"Can you wait outside?"

He huffed and had to stop himself from laughing out loud. "I'm not going anywhere, sweetheart." Lord walked over to the examination table where her legs were now dangling over the side, the sheet pulled up high. "Despite what you think, I wasn't involved in any of this. And our deal is still in full effect."

"So, your own club members beat me half to death and humiliate me, but I'm still required to be your sex slave for God knows how long?"

He shrugged a shoulder.

She continued. "Oh, right. The alternative is getting murdered by you for my father's lack of loyalty."

At least she had some fire. He'd hated seeing her broken and afraid to speak.

"You have a good memory. Now get dressed," he said. "Or you can walk to my room naked, if you prefer."

She glared at him and it made his cock firm up. In his world, women never challenged him, and he found her little tantrums arousing. If she wasn't so banged up, he'd spank her ass. Within minutes, she'd managed to pull on the shirt and sweatpants without exposing an inch of skin. He did notice how she cringed when lifting her arms over her head. That deep-seated rage started to boil up again, but he pushed it down. He needed to show Ally his softer side, if he even had one, and keep his anger in check. His club members would be schooled tonight, and he sure as hell didn't mind showing those responsible his darker side.

"I'm ready." She stood in front of him now, trying to put on a brave face. He saw right through her. Ally was hanging on by a thread.

He held the door open and followed her out.

Tarmac approached them from the opposite end

of the hallway, Righteous close behind him. "Boss, we need to talk."

"We will. Tonight, in church. Unless it's life or death, I don't want to hear about it before then. Understand?"

Tarmac nodded, but Lord knew something was brewing with the Skull Nation. He was eager to deal with those motherfuckers himself, but Ally was going to come first. There was always a rival banging on their doors, but only one of her. He had to start doing things right and make amends if he wanted a future with the busty little blonde.

Ally stared at the ground until the brothers walked past them. One day, she'd walk these halls like a queen, her head held high. Just the thought of it made his world feel whole, so he knew claiming her had to be a good decision. His intuition always steered him in the right direction.

After entering his bedroom and closing the door, Ally turned to face him. "You can't protect me, Lord. You can't be by my side every minute of every day. This will only happen again," she said. "So, your end of the deal is already null and void."

He combed both his hands into her hair, gently securing her head so she couldn't look away. "Today was never supposed to happen. I plan to make sure every single member of my club knows my intentions. No one will ever lay a finger on you again. I promise you that."

Her eyes were flooded with unshed tears. The girl was stubborn. But he'd been an asshole, and he knew it.

"You can't make that promise."

"Do you know who I am, Ally?"

She swallowed hard, unable to look away.

"Say it," he said.

"The president of the Straight to Hell MC."

Lord nodded. "That's right. And once everyone knows how important you are, they'll treat you like gold. No one here will hurt you. I'll never hurt you."

****

Ally wasn't sure what to think or say. This was like a fucked-up fairy tale, and she didn't know what to make of it. She expected to wake up to her alarm clock, and this entire ordeal was all a nightmare.

But then she'd never have met Lord.

Would that be a good or bad thing?

Her heart kept tugging, insisting there was something worth exploring between them. But then he'd turn into an asshole and make her question everything.

"I'm not important," she said.

"You are."

She scoffed. He'd made it clear he was only keeping her alive because he wanted her virginity. She was a toy, his plaything of the week. And she had no doubt he could get any woman he wanted. Not only was he the prez, but he had an irresistible dark masculinity that held her captive. His scars, his flaws, his rough personality—it all added to his appeal.

"You don't believe me?" he asked.

"You have a short memory. I thought … I thought things were going in a different direction last night, then this morning you were like a different person. I don't know who you are, and you don't know who I am. We're strangers."

"I know."

"And then your own people attacked me. Humiliated me. I've never felt confident about myself, but today was the lowest I've ever felt." Her traitorous tears slipped down her cheeks. She wanted desperately to be strong, to overcome her insecurities, to appear unaffected. It was impossible.

He kept silent, holding her head in place with his big, strong hands. Did he think she was weak? She was nothing like the women in his club, and she never would be.

"I'm sorry," he whispered.

The sincerity in his gruff voice pushed her over the edge, deep waves of sorrow rocking her body. He pulled her against his hard body, holding her as she cried against him. It hurt her ribs a bit, but she didn't care. She desperately needed his comfort and affection. Without him, she'd be alone in the world. At the mercy of the club.

"This morning, I was trying to push you away. Trying to be an asshole."

"Why?"

"It's what I do," he said. "I'm not used to caring about a woman. Emotions are dangerous in a place like this."

She believed him. The men in the club were like sharks. Ally had no doubt they'd tear apart anyone showing a weakness. What she couldn't believe was that his feelings for her had changed so quickly.

"You said this was a deal. A temporary thing."

"And that's what I wanted it to be. Until I didn't."

She bit her lower lip, wondering, hoping.

He kept talking in riddles, and she wondered if he was just as insecure as her. He'd had a brutal childhood and a rough life in the MC. Trust wouldn't come easy for him. Hell, it didn't come easy for her.

"Lord." She looked up at him, resting a hand on his bicep. He flinched for a moment, his muscles tensing. "Tell me what you want from me. *Really* want from me."

He started to pull away again, but she held on to his sleeve.

"I don't know, Ally. My life was just fine until

you came along. Now, I don't know what the fuck to think." He took a breath. "I want more."

"More?"

"I'm forty years old. The other brothers are fine fucking club pussy every night. They're in heaven. It's what they want," he said. "It's what I should want."

"And now?" She held her breath.

"Now I want more. A worthy woman—innocent, sweet, mine. A virgin only I get to fuck. Kids. Nights watching movies. Feeling happy."

"Sounds nice."

"Does it?"

"I'm scared, Lord. Scared of being in a motorcycle club, of getting hurt again, of having my heart broken."

"What about me, Ally? Am I a monster to you? Are you counting the days until I cut you loose?"

She shook her head, and before she could speak, his lips were on hers. He cupped the sides of her head, kissing deeply, desperately, as if his life depended on this one kiss. She was lost.

Falling, falling, falling.

When her knees grew weak, he scooped her up into his arms, effortlessly carrying her over to his big bed. He set her down, not breaking the kiss right away.

He rested a knee on the mattress. "If I let you leave right now, no debt, no retaliation, will you walk?"

She shrugged. "What life is there for me here?"

"One with me. By my side."

"I'm not naïve. I know how it works in an MC. I couldn't stand sharing you, wondering if you're screwing around with one of the women around here."

"Ally, If I claim you, you're the only woman I'll ever have eyes for. Just before my mother passed away, I remember swearing I'd never hurt my old lady the way she'd been hurt. It's not who I am."

"Old lady?"

"One day. That's the goal, right?"

She wanted to belong to him, to belong *period*. Living on her own, pinching pennies, having no support system, it wasn't an easy life. Love was a distant thought, something she never dreamed to obtain. If anything, she expected to be used by men, have her heart broken time and time again. From what she'd seen at the bar, most men were cheaters, and that was one thing her heart couldn't take.

"Everyone here hates me."

He smirked. His beard was coming in thicker. The way he looked at her brought her body to life, even though it had been broken earlier.

"Everyone will worship every step you take after tonight. We're having a meeting, and I'll set the club straight. It won't be a problem."

"What will you tell them?"

She wanted him to take ownership of her, to make her his old lady. But they'd only been together such a short time, and it was too soon. It didn't stop her from wanting it, though. She worried he'd tire of her, change his mind once he got to know the real her.

"That you're mine. And if anyone lays a finger on you, they'll answer directly to me."

Ally licked her lips. Right now, she wished her body wasn't achy and bruised. She wanted Lord all over her, his hands and mouth exploring every inch of her body. Even without their deal, she wanted him to have her virginity. Any other man would be a disappointment in comparison to Lord. He was all male, powerful, no holds barred, and apparently, he wanted her.

He trailed a finger along her cheek, down her neck, and over the swell of her breast. Her heart raced, her pussy throbbing. She breathed in shallow gasps, anticipating his next move.

He rested his forehead against hers. "Don't ever feel ashamed of this body. Those club whores aren't even in your league, baby girl. They give themselves away for free. You're different. You're all mine."

She remembered how they'd taunted her. They reminded her of how fat and out of shape she was—a waste of space, covered in cellulite, worthless garbage. It had been an excruciating experience emotionally. How could the prez choose someone like her? Her self-esteem was so shattered, it was hard to accept any positive words from him.

"You could do better."

He narrowed his eyes. "I'm partially to blame for his bullshit. I shouldn't have tried to push you away, but it sure as hell wasn't because I thought I could do better," he said. "I went to that farm to kill you, but one look at you, and I fell hard. One fucking look and I was a goner. That doesn't happen. It took me by surprise, and I didn't like feeling weak. But this body of yours is all I can think about. You're all woman. Perfect."

"You've barely touched me."

He wet his thick lips, turning her on even more. "And I won't. Not until these bruises have faded and your hand's healed."

She didn't want to wait that long. But the fact he'd hold off for her benefit made her feel special.

"And then what will you do to me?"

"I plan to fuck you raw, little girl. I'll have you begging me for cock. I may be an ugly motherfucker, but when I'm done with you, I promise you won't care."

Chapter Seven

Lord had hoped Ally would finally believe him and allow herself time to relax around the club. Two weeks later, though, he knew she wasn't going to give him the chance to prove anything.

They'd all decided on a barbeque for dinner tonight. A couple of the club pussy had gone with some of the guys to the store, grabbing meat and vegetables to throw onto the grill. A buffet table was set up, and music filled the air but not too loud that conversation couldn't be heard.

He watched Ally. She didn't try to make any kind of run for it. Not for the last two weeks. And not today. Whenever he got to his room, she was always sound asleep, curled up in the corner of the bed.

The bruises had mostly faded away. He didn't like the way she kept a wall up between them. How long was he expected to wait?

The night she'd been attacked, he'd called church and made sure everyone knew what it meant if they messed with Ally. He forced them all to realize she was important to him, and not to fucking mess with her. There was no way in hell he'd entertain a replay of what happened two weeks ago, and everyone knew it.

With the fact he'd already killed one of the whores and buried her, the women had fallen in line. None of the old ladies were present tonight. They hadn't hung around the club much. From what he could see, Ally tended to help with cleaning up after parties, and then she'd take her seat outside and watch the sun set.

Like now, she had a plate in front of her filled with food, but he'd yet to see her eat anything. Maybe taking a civilian as his woman would never work.

She ran her fork across everything, without

pronging it. Would she ever accept life in the club?

"You okay?" Brick asked.

He'd been asking that question an awful lot lately, and Lord was tired of it.

"Why the fuck wouldn't I be?"

"You're staring at that chick real hard. She's your property, man. Go over there and tell her what it's all about."

Lord looked at Brick. He trusted the man more than anyone else. It was why he'd made him VP, why he was willing to listen to him.

"What have the boys been saying?" he asked, taking a bite of his burger.

"About what?"

"About anything." He didn't care what they thought of his leadership skills. All he cared about was what they thought of Ally.

"They think you're pussy whipped. They're curious about her, that's about it. None of them have anything else to say otherwise." Brick shrugged. "It's hard for them to understand. Pussy is pussy, Lord. What makes her so different?"

He watched Ally. She put her fork down to tuck some hair behind her ear. She stared across the yard, not making eye contact with anyone, forever in a daze. He'd already gotten a full background check on her and there was nothing about her life that she would miss. No one waiting for her. She had a couple of friends, but from what he'd read, they were so hung up on their own lives they didn't give a shit about the friend who never called back.

Gripping the back of his neck, he frowned as he watched her.

She was really something.

Beautiful.

Sweet.

Kind.

That was what he'd gotten from the information, and it seemed hard to believe she was Richard's daughter. The pain he'd heard in her voice after she'd been attacked, he'd wanted to take it all away. To protect her. He'd never wanted to help anyone.

Ally was different. No doubt about that.

He swallowed the last of his beer, tossed the bottle into the trashcan, and made his way over to her.

"That food isn't going to yell at you if you eat it," he said.

Her brow rose. "I'm not very hungry."

"You haven't been very hungry for two weeks."

"I guess this place is the best diet I've been on." She pressed her lips together. He wanted to force-feed her, but instead, he held his hand out.

She frowned at his hand.

"Come on," he said.

"I'm fine, thank you."

"I'm not asking permission, princess. I can make you, and you will follow my orders."

She looked like she wanted to throw her food at him, but instead, she put her plate on her chair and stood. She wore a pair of sweatpants and the ugliest shirt he'd ever seen. None of it highlighted her feminine curves. It was like she was trying to hide from him, but he wasn't going to give her the satisfaction of doing that.

Sliding his arm around her waist, he pulled her close. Her soft curves felt like heaven as they pressed against him.

The music turned up even louder. He didn't care that it was a heavy beat and not the kind to slow dance to.

"You don't believe I can take care of you," he

said.

"I haven't said anything."

"And you're always sitting so far away, Ally. Why is that?"

She sighed and her gaze moved to his shoulder. "You can try to force your club to like me, Lord, but … they don't. People whisper and they're saying you killed someone for me. I didn't ask for that."

"I didn't kill anyone for you." The lie fell easily from his lips.

She tensed in his arms. "I'm not a child. You don't need to keep treating me like one."

"I'm not."

"Yes, you are." She tilted her head back to look at him. "I'm not stupid. You lie so easily to me. You want to know why I can't believe what you say. Can you even believe it?" She pulled out of his arms. "Thank you for the dance."

She surprised him even more by grabbing her plate and throwing it in the trash. They were paper plates. No one liked doing the dishes after a nice barbeque feast.

He ran his hand through his hair and grit his teeth.

Lord wasn't done with this conversation. Without looking at his men, he followed Ally into the clubhouse. She wasn't in the kitchen, nor in the main room. It meant she'd already made her escape to his bedroom, which only served to piss him off.

She didn't have to keep on hiding. The fact she didn't believe him spoke volumes to him. He would've hurt anyone else who dared to question his authority.

No woman had him chasing after them.

It seemed he was constantly making exceptions when it came to Ally, which he didn't fucking like.

Charging upstairs, he saw his bedroom was empty but the bathroom door was open. He walked in to find Ally already undressed. The shower was running and she tried to cover her body, but he'd already seen her completely naked. He wasn't disappointed.

"What are you doing?" she asked.

He walked right toward her, forcing her to take several steps back as he advanced until her back finally hit the wall, stopping her progress.

"You're scaring me," she said.

"No, I'm not." He slammed his hands at either side of her head, trapping her between his body and the wall. "I've told you I won't hurt you, and anything I do to you, you're going to want."

"I want to go home."

"Well, you're not getting that," he said.

"Because you reneged on our deal and I'm not supposed to be here. I hate it here. I want to go home, and I don't care how much that makes me sound like a child, it's true."

He stared at her. He liked that she still had fire. At least she was speaking to him, getting it all out.

Most women wanted to please him, not Ally.

He stroked her cheek, and she tensed up. There were still shadows of bruises on her face and body. Making a decision, he lifted her up, tossing her over his shoulder. She let out a cry. "Put me down."

He did on the edge of the bed, where he spread her legs, exposing her sweet pussy to him. Her virgin cunt. He placed his hands on her inner thighs, keeping her open to him.

"What are you doing?"

"What I should have done the first night you were fucking here." Pressing his face against her pussy, he licked and sucked at her clit, tasting her sweet virgin cunt for the first time. Damn, she was even better than he imagined. He'd never been the kind of man to eat pussy before, but he knew he was going to be spending a lot of time between Ally's spread thighs. She was the best thing he'd ever tasted. After one lick of her, he wanted more.

Sliding his tongue back and forth across her clit, he glanced up to find her eyes closed. Her hands gripped the bedsheets tightly as if her life depended on it.

She was such a beautiful sight.

His cock was unbearably hard as he watched her, tasted her. He wanted to hear her come.

With her distracted, he opened the top button of his pants, sliding the zipper down. He'd stop if she asked, but tonight, she was going to belong to him.

****

Heaven.

Ally had no idea someone's tongue could feel so amazing. She'd watched a few porno movies and seen a man going down on a woman, but she'd never given much thought as to how it would feel to have a man licking her between the thighs.

It was a heady experience. One she didn't want to stop.

Even when he used his teeth to a point of almost too much pain, she didn't want him to stop. Holding on to the bed as if it was a lifeline was all she could do.

"You have the nicest pussy I've ever eaten."

His words found her through the fog of arousal, the gruffness of his voice making her nipples tighten. His tongue flicked back and forth across her clit. Any coherent thought was lost to her on a wave of overwhelming need. She couldn't stop the way she was feeling, nor did she want to. He was filthy and she loved every minute of it.

"Please," she said.

She felt desperate, wanton, and needed to jump

off this precipice.

"Come for me, Ally. I want to hear you scream for it." She did as he asked and came hard.

Her entire body was thrust into shockwaves of pleasure so intense it shook her to the core. She hadn't even finished enjoying this heady sense of release when Lord moved over her. He didn't go far as he settled between her spread thighs. The tip of his cock traced along her wet slit. He was going to take her.

She knew it.

His frame was huge and he smelled so damn good.

Part of her wanted him to stop, but the other part of her didn't. She'd never been considered desirable and as he looked at her, she felt this pull. Lord not only wanted her, he craved her. He was like a man possessed in his need for her.

She didn't tell him to stop, even as fear started to rush through her body at the feel of his hard cock.

Lord wasn't small. His cock was poised at her entrance and she knew he wouldn't be gentle.

"You're all mine now, Ally." He thrust hard. Pain erupted as he slid in balls deep.

She cried out. Gripping his shoulders, her nails sank into the flesh, trying to throw him off but to also keep him inside.

He didn't stop. His cock kept pushing in deep.

She felt like she was being torn in two before he finally seated himself to the hilt within her, pausing, holding himself still.

The vision of him swam as tears filled her eyes. She tried to breathe through the pain, but it didn't help.

Lord leaned down close, his lips brushing across her ear. "I'm sorry," he said.

She wondered if he was used to apologizing. At

that moment, she couldn't even remember if he'd apologized for the way his men and women had attacked her.

Slowly, the pain that had sliced through her began to ebb away. Lord pulled back, still within her.

He'd been fully dressed. She didn't know how he'd gotten his jeans off.

"I didn't want to hurt you," he said. "I never had a virgin. Thought hard and quick would be best."

"It wasn't."

He continued to stare at her.

"Do you always break your promises?"

"Ally, I'm going to protect and take care of you. You can trust me."

"My bruises haven't all faded." It was a poor excuse, as most of them had been. She wasn't in pain. The few pulled ligaments had started to feel fine again. Staring up at him as the pain lessened, she didn't hate him.

Lord was used to taking what he wanted.

Even as she wanted him, she'd also been afraid that the moment he got what he wanted, he'd pass her over. Without her virginity, would he even want her for much longer? She didn't want to be cast aside and forgotten.

"Does it still hurt?" he asked.

She shook her head. "No."

"Good, you can hate me all you want, Ally. I wasn't responsible for my men or the bitches doing what they did. I will pay for their sins, but I'm not giving you up. I haven't reneged on our deal once. You belong to me, and since you're alive and breathing, I'm doing a damn good job." He pulled out of her and she tensed up, but he stopped.

His hand moved to cup her cheek and he came

close to her. His lips a mere breath away. She could almost taste him.

Ally watched, waited. His tongue traced across her bottom lip and she gasped at the sudden contact. He kissed her as he pressed forward and she opened her mouth to receive him.

He released a groan as he kissed her.

At first, she didn't know what to do. She hadn't kissed him back.

"I don't mind if you don't want to kiss me, but I've been told I'm not too bad at kissing."

She jerked back and glared at him. "Don't talk to me about what you do with other women. I don't want to hear about them, and I certainly don't want to know what you do with them."

He started to laugh. "Babe, I want you to kiss me back. Believe it or not, I haven't kissed any of the women here. I know where their mouths have been, and I'm not interested in sucking one of my men's cocks."

"That wasn't very nice."

"The image of me sucking a man's cock?"

"No, making me think there were other women you've kissed."

He sighed. "I'm balls deep inside of you, but I'm not going to lie to you, Ally, I've been with plenty of the women who frequent here. I'm not a saint."

"I know that, but I don't have to know details, do I?" She looked at him, wanting to demand some exclusivity, but at the same time, feeling so far out of her depth, she didn't know what to say or do. Instead, she kept her thoughts to herself.

"I won't say anything. Now, can I actually fuck you and prove to you it's not all pain?"

She nodded, and as he started to move, she tensed up. She couldn't help it.

He let out a curse, but rather than stop, he began to slowly rock in and out of her. Ally expected pain, but there was none. Staring up into his eyes, she watched him. Lord stopped all of a sudden and reached between them. His fingers stroked over her clit.

She didn't think it could be possible for her to feel any kind of arousal, but as his fingers worked their magic, he proved to her she really didn't know what she was doing as another wave of arousal flooded her.

"That's it, baby. Fuck, it feels good on my cock. That's how I want you, wet and willing. I want you to forget about the pain. It's never going to hurt again. You might be a little sore, but nothing bad, I promise."

To answer, she moaned his name as he moved within her at the same time as he worked her clit.

"I want you to take over. Touch yourself," he said. He took her hand and licked her fingers, getting them nice and slick before he placed them between her thighs. She gasped and he grinned. "I'm going to make you feel so good."

She didn't think it was possible to feel any better, but as she began to stroke her swollen clit, he once again proved that he knew what he was doing. His hands went to her hips, and he began to rock inside her, going deeper as she worked her clit.

The pain was completely gone as he started to fuck her harder. She wanted to come again. Sinking her teeth into her lip, she arched up, taking his cock.

She wished she could feel him skin to skin, his big, hard muscles pressed to her naked body. But this was about lust, taking her fast and hard. Getting her virginity out of the way.

"That's it, baby. I want you to come for me. Let me have it."

She cried out his name as her second orgasm took

her completely by surprise. Lord held her down as he began to fuck her. The pleasure continued as Lord made her his.

When he came, she felt every pulse of his cock as it filled her pussy, flooding her with his cum.

Lord collapsed over her and it was so natural to her to stroke his head as he rested against her. Whether it was just sex or not, there was something bonding about it. At least she could feel a new connection.

The only sounds in the room were of their labored breathing. She closed her eyes.

She was no longer a virgin.

Lord had taken care of that.

She'd always imagined her first time being with someone she loved, maybe even on her wedding night. So stupid of her to think such sweet things when her life had been anything but.

"I left the shower running," she said.

"I just fucked you and all you can think about is the shower?" Lord asked, laughing. "Where the fuck have you been all my life?"

Her heart jumped at his words. Did he want to know her? Like really know her?

Lord lifted up and looked down at her. "Are you okay?"

She had so many questions and was so confused. There was no place for her to start, so she smiled at him. "I'm fine." She hated lying, but in this situation, she didn't feel she could offer any other kind of answer. What was there to say? Her feelings for him were confusing her. He'd taken her virginity and she'd wanted him to have it.

He cupped her cheek, and the action was so tender, she found herself holding her breath, waiting.

Lord was not a gentle man.

He was all darkness. He'd warned her of this many times.

Looking at him now, she had to wonder if she had made a deal with the devil. If she really had, there was no way she was getting out of this alive. He was going to own every part of her—mind, body, and soul.

Chapter Eight

Lord shook out his hand after punching the bastard in the face again. Reaper caught the man's body when it fell back, pushing him toward Lord for more punishment.

"Every name," said Lord. "Not one. Not two. All of them."

"I told you what I know." The Skull Nation prick could barely see out of one eye, blood dripping from his swollen nose. And he was lying.

Lord punched him again. This time, a gold tooth went flying across the room.

The Skull Nation had attempted to drive them out of their northern tourist towns. They were highly profitable and Lord had let it go on long enough. He had no plans on handing over the hard-earned territory to their rivals. The Skull Nation boys had killed a few of their whores and a couple of brothers. They'd taken over one of the brothels and were attempting to control the drug trade in and out of the small towns.

Tonight, Lord rode into town with Tarmac, Brick, Reaper, Stump, and a few other brothers. Ally had been behind him, her hands under his shirt as she held on tight.

His first stop was a hotel where he set up Ally in one of the best rooms. He needed to know she was safe while he handled business. Lord ordered two brothers to guard the place. He wasn't taking any chances when it came to her.

Brick had tried to convince him to leave Ally back home at the compound, but he wasn't comfortable leaving that many miles between them. Especially when this was going to take more than a couple of days to clean up.

"Reaper, this motherfucker is testing my

patience," said Lord.

"I can get him to talk, boss. Just say the word."

Lord paced in the abandoned warehouse, back and forth, his hands clasped behind his back. They'd already assembled all the Straight to Hell members in the area and had begun to take back the towns, one Skull Nation asshole at a time.

But this went deeper. He needed the names of the men in charge of this infiltration. He had a couple, but not close to all. Lord wanted every man responsible for stepping on his territory to pay the ultimate price.

"Handle this," said Lord. "I'll head over to the whorehouse with Brick."

They made a lot of money off women. All were in the brothels by choice. They enjoyed working their way up the ranks in the club, but they were supposed to be protected. They were already losing longtime customers with all the killing and upheaval. It was time to set things straight.

Lord and his VP rode out to the brothel. Several Straight to Hell brothers from town were waiting for them.

"How did this get so out of control?" Lord asked Stitch. He was one of the brothers living close to town.

"They must have been planning this a long time."

"No, it should have been dealt with the second you found out about it. One bullet could have stopped this before it turned into this clusterfuck. I'm starting to wonder where your loyalties lie."

"Lord, I'll do better. I swear."

"And you." He diverted his attention to Gabriel, one of the first members to alert Lord to the takeover. "Why the fuck haven't you gotten a handle on this yet?"

"We're outnumbered. We were waiting for backup, but I guess you were busy with your new girl," said Gabriel.

Lord grabbed him around the neck, squeezing enough that the asshole knew he wasn't playing. "Don't talk about my woman. And don't assume anything. Your job is to protect our investments in this piece-of-shit town. If you can't handle it, you don't deserve to wear this cut. Understand?" He pushed Gabriel back.

"I'll clean this town up. The Skull Nation will regret showing their faces here."

"We have local cops on our payroll. Guard this fucking brothel like your life depends on it. It does. If anyone from the Skull Nation sets foot in this town, don't play games. Put them under the ground."

Stitch nodded. As did Gabriel and Whisky.

Lord tapped Brick and they entered the brothel. The whores looked shocked to see him enter the grand foyer. He never handled the day-to-day operations of their businesses and rarely paid a visit. He ran a hand through his hair, the leather of his jacket creaking. "Are there any Skull Nation boys in here?"

Two younger whores, barely dressed, pointed up the stairs. They looked terrified of him.

Brick grabbed one of the girls by the arm, making her yelp. "Next time one of them tries to come in here, you call us. If I find out you're fucking our enemies, you'll be out on the streets. Or worse."

They made their way up the winding staircase. Lord had his handgun at the ready.

One of the regular whores came down the hall. He put a finger to his lips.

She knew right away what he wanted and pointed to the second door on the left. Lord smiled, knowing he was so close, and motioned her to get away.

They flanked the door. When Lord nodded, Brick kicked in the door. Two women were on the bed, a Skull

Nation prick between them.

"Get the fuck out!" he yelled at the sluts. They'd be dealt with later.

Brick stood at the opposite side of the bed as the Skull Nation guy covered his cock with the blankets. He put up an arm in surrender.

Brick laughed. "You think our prez does mercy? You have some huge fucking balls coming to *our* whorehouse in *our* town."

"Did you think I'd let this continue forever?" asked Lord. He checked the chamber of his gun.

"You smoke me, there'll be war."

"You supposed to be important?" asked Brick. "You look like any other dead man."

"I'm the Skull Nation Road Captain."

"Will you look at that. Royalty right in my own fucking house," said Lord. Then he reached over and dragged him violently out of the bed by the hair, the blanket falling away. "If you think your status is supposed to impress me, you're a stupid fucking boy. This is my town. I'm prez of the Straight to Hell MC."

"And he doesn't do mercy," said Brick.

The guy tried to fight him, but Lord was built like a brick shithouse. Hours in the gym every day and a life built in the MC made him a brutal motherfucker. He punched him in the face, knocking him back. Over and over, they sparred, the guy's face bleeding and swollen. Brick stood on the sidelines, not saying a word.

"We know about Ally," he said as he tried to get back up to his feet.

Lord yanked him up. "What did you just say?"

He laughed, his teeth red with blood. "How did you think we were able to take over this town? You're too busy chasing pussy to realize how weak you've become. You're a has-been."

Lord beat the shit out of him, not holding back. "How do you know her name?" he shouted. "Tell me now or I'll put a bullet in your head."

"You shouldn't trust everyone in your house." He laughed again.

This time, he pulled his gun from the back of his waistband and put the barrel to the fucker's temple. "See you in hell." Then he pulled the trigger.

This was usual MC business. Protecting territory was a full-time job, always had been, always would be. Lord wasn't shaken by the Skull Nation making a play because he'd deal with it as he always did.

What he wasn't expecting was to hear Ally's name on his enemy's lips. She wasn't supposed to be involved at all. The worlds were colliding and it didn't sit well with him.

He didn't realize how long he stood there next to the body, his mind lost in thought.

"Boss, he's just screwing with you."

Lord shook his head. "He knew her fucking name."

"She's safe."

"He said there's a traitor in the club. Any ideas?"

"Someone selling inside information? I'll have to dig deeper."

He took a deep breath to calm himself. All he wanted to do was get back to Ally and see with his own eyes that she was safe and unharmed.

"I want this piece of shit thrown out on the main roadway. He'll send a message as we finish cleaning up this town."

They left the room. Lord was more shaken up than he realized. He couldn't focus.

"Lord, how serious are you about this girl? You know more than anyone that having a loved one is a huge target. Our enemies prey on your weaknesses, and they'll use her against you. It's already starting."

"You think I'd put her over the good of the club?"

Brick shrugged. "You've known her less than a month. I'm just saying to make sure she's worth it."

****

Ally looked out the window again. It was getting late.

She was lonely and worried about Lord. At least he'd brought her along. It would have been worse being alone at the club where everyone hated her. She didn't feel safe without Lord around.

It had been nearly a week since he'd taken her virginity. At least he hadn't dumped her. She'd been worried that was all he wanted from their arrangement.

He'd been in meetings all week with his club. She could feel the tension. This rival club was infiltrating their turf, and now Lord was going to deal with it. Yes, she worried about him. What if he never came back to her?

From what she'd seen so far, people either hated him or feared him. He had a rough personality. And probably deserved what he got out of people. With her, he behaved differently. She saw the good in him, and he probably needed that.

He said he wanted to keep her rather than fulfilling their original terms. Lord wanted her for more than a plaything now, but for how long? Was she a new pet or was the MC prez capable of real love?

When she heard the familiar sound of bike engines purring, the sound carried all the way down to her pussy. It reminded her of Lord. She couldn't see any bikes from the window, so she hoped it was him finally returning to her.

Minutes later, there was a scuffle in the hallway. The walls seemed to shudder as bodies were rammed against them. She didn't dare open the door, even though her nerves and curiosity were driving her crazy.

The sound of more bikes stole her attention. She rushed back over to the window. This time, she was certain it was Lord approaching the hotel with a few other bikes alongside him. Her heart beat frantically in her chest. Who was in the hallway?

Maybe it was just some drunk.

Silence finally returned to her room … followed by a knock at her door. There was no way it was Lord already. He was still on the road outside.

"Open the door, Ally."

She bit her lip. He knew her name, but she didn't recognize the voice at all. Ally paced back and forth, finally deciding to ignore the constant knocking.

When he began pounding on it, the frame buckling, panic set in. He was trying to break in, which had to mean he was one of Lord's enemies. She looked side to side, unable to catch her breath. In a last-ditch effort, she locked herself inside the bathroom, keeping as quiet as possible.

The door burst open, slapping against the wall behind it. "Ally?"

She hated hearing him say her name. The same fear she'd felt when that cop kidnapped her and locked her in his trunk came back with a vengeance. This would probably end up much worse. The Skull Nation would want to make an example of her, to rub her violent death in Lord's face.

Please hurry up and get upstairs.

The knob of the bathroom door rattled. She didn't move a muscle. Within seconds, he'd picked the basic lock and opened the door, flicking on the light. Ally sat there on the closed toilet with no way to defend herself, completely cornered.

"Oh, thank God." He exhaled and rested a hand against the wall. "You're okay."

She relaxed somewhat.

"My name's Whisky. I work for Lord."

"What's going on?"

"Three guys were trying to break in your room. If I hadn't stopped them, Lord would have had my head."

"Where are they now?"

"Still in the hallway."

She hadn't heard any gunshots, but she didn't dare ask for details. They were likely dead, but she didn't need to know.

"Thank you," she said.

"I'm just glad you're okay. You are okay, eh?"

Ally nodded, the relief making her limbs feel heavy. Her pulse lowered, her breathing returning to normal.

"Where the fuck is she?" the voice bellowed in her hotel room.

Whisky rushed away from her. "In the bathroom," he said.

Lord's heavy footfalls came closer. He looked like the devil himself, immediately lifting her up to her feet. "What happened? Are you hurt?"

"Whisky saved me. Strangers were trying to break in my room."

"Not strangers. Skull Nation. Brick was right, it's too dangerous keeping a woman," he said. "They'll never stop using you against me."

She narrowed her eyes, not liking where this was going. The thought of losing Lord was just too much.

"Whisky, how'd they get up here? Why weren't they stopped before coming in the building?"

"There were three of them. They knew exactly where they were going and took the stairs. I got one in the lobby, and was right behind the other two," said Whisky. "No way was I letting them in this room."

"Good work. You can head out now that I'm here. Just deal with those bodies." Lord set his handgun on the nightside table, then shrugged off his leather jacket. Whisky and Lord's other men filed out of the room, pulling the broken door closed behind them.

He sat on the edge of the bed once they were alone and scrubbed his hands over his face, leaning over his knees.

"Lord, they never got to me. Everything's fine."

He ignored her, shaking his head as he stood up, walking back and forth in front of her. "When a prez or high rank has an old lady, it's a weakness for the entire club. I never thought about the consequences of keeping you. I'm supposed to put the good of the club before everything else."

"So, you're not allowed to be happy? You can never have a family?"

He stopped pacing and cupped her face. "When it was my own club that hurt you, I dealt with it. It was in my control. This shit is different. The Skull Nation knows who you are. I don't know how yet, but they do. This isn't just about the safety of the club, it's about protecting *you*."

A new desperation crept up on her. She couldn't lose Lord, not when her heart already beat his name. They'd just started their unorthodox love story.

"So, what are you saying, Lord? You're done with me? You took my virginity and played with my heart, and now I'm too dangerous to keep?" She pulled away and turned her back to him. No way would she beg him, not after everything she'd endured.

"Ally, you know it's not like that," he said. "You want to live your life looking over your shoulder? I can't be with you every second of every day."

"What about Whisky? He saved me. He was there. So why are you worried?"

He stood up straight, his expression hard.

"I should have been the one to save you, Ally. Not Whisky, not anyone."

"They're your men, doing your bidding. Same thing, Lord."

"It's not."

"Whatever, you manage your whorehouses and do your thing. I'm sure your bed will always be warmed by club whores. Nobody wants to murder them. I'll just get the hell out of your life. It's easier for you that way." Her emotions were bubbling up all over the place. She was a mess, an angry, bitter mess.

She was about to storm out and make the necessary dramatic exit, but he grabbed her arm to keep her in place. "I don't want this, Ally. But Brick was right."

"Brick is alone and miserable. He'll die alone because he doesn't believe in love."

"He seems happy. He's popular with the women," Lord said.

"Women who sleep with half the club don't count. You're all so shallow. Nothing is real in your world. I thought what we had might be different. I was wrong."

He pulled her against his chest, whispering into her hair. "I wanted to be the one to save you, not Whisky."

"I don't care about him, Lord. I've been wishing you were here all night. I miss you every time you're gone."

His hands tightened in her hair. "I thought it would be easier to cut you loose. You've only been in my life for the blink of an eye. But it's fucking hard. I don't know why."

She hoped it was love, some connection deeper than sex and control.

"I want to be with you," she said. "You're all I have now."

Even though her father wasn't a factor in her life, Lord had turned everything upside down. She had no apartment or job to go back to now. She was completely immersed in his life. His club.

She ran her hands down his chest. He was such a presence, such strength and raw masculinity. The scent of his cologne aroused her. Everything about him turned her on. He didn't scare her, in fact, he made her feel protected and safe.

Ally curled her fingers around his thick leather belt.

Could he read her mind? Did he know what she wanted from him?

Right now, she needed security, reassurance, love. But she'd settle for sex. All she wanted was to feel desired by Lord, connected in any way possible.

"I've never cared about a woman until you. You've fucked with my head."

"You're allowed to have a life, Lord. Does the club always have to come first?" She slid her hand under his shirt, feeling his warm, firm skin.

"That's the problem, baby. If I had to choose, I'd choose you over anything. Even my club."

Her breath caught. For a man like Lord, that was even more powerful than saying he loved her. The room sounded quieter than a morgue.

"Then don't push me away." She wrapped her

arms around his neck, kissing his jawline, one kiss after the other. "Promise me."

"I promise," he said just before his lips came down over hers. Lord kissed her thoroughly, making time stand still. He began to lift her shirt up, only breaking their kiss long enough to pull the shirt over her head.

"I need you, Lord." She tilted her head to the side as he trailed kisses down her neck.

"Whisky saved you today, but I'm your man, Ally. Don't forget that. This body belongs to me."

She wet her lips. "Make sure I don't forget."

Chapter Nine

Lord stared out across the compound. His woman sat on the small patch of grass toward the back, reading a book. With all of his business, she'd been complaining of being bored. Rather than allow her to hate her life here, he'd made one of his boys go to the local bookstore and buy as many titles as they could get their hands on. Now as he watched, she had a small pile of books beside her.

She looked so fucking cute.

Running a hand down his face, he hated this. Hated the indecision. He'd gone back to the hotel with the sole intention of getting rid of her.

What had he done instead? Kept her. With a traitor close.

He didn't know why he needed to keep her. Sure, her pussy had never been touched by another man, and her devotion to him was highly addictive, but keeping her made him look weak.

The one thing he hated more than anything was to look weak. In his world, he'd already cost himself so much.

"Is everything okay?" Brick asked.

"Yes. Any word?"

"So far The Skull Nation is lying low. No sign of them."

Lord shook his head. "That's not good. When they're lying low, that means they're planning something."

"What do you think it is?"

"Either a full-on assault so long as they can get the numbers, or something else." Again, he looked outside at his woman. She was too sweet for him. The biggest mistake he'd made was thinking they stood a chance.

"They try to attack here, we've got it covered," Brick said.

"I'm not going to wait around for them to attack," Lord said. "We've got too many businesses demanding our attention. They could just wait us out." The Skull Nation were not good people. If they got ahold of Ally, that would be it. They would make her wish he'd killed her to spare her the pain of what they would do. Just thinking about what they could do to her filled him with a rage he knew all too well. Only this came from a feeling deep within, attached to a little part for Ally alone.

"Do you want me to grab the boys for a meeting?" Brick asked.

"Tonight. We plan." He turned toward Brick. "I've got to handle something first."

He left his office, making his way outside to where Ally read. Since he'd looked at her from his office, she'd move to lay spread out across the grass. Her legs were crossed at the ankles as she lifted the book up in the air. She flicked over a page at the same time as tucking some of her hair behind her ear.

"Good book?"

She turned toward him with a smile.

That look in her eyes, it was what he wanted every single day.

She turned the book over and got to her feet, rushing toward him. He captured her in his arms as she threw herself at him. Such youth and sweet innocence. He was addicted to her love. And he didn't deserve any of it.

"I haven't seen you all morning." She kissed his cheek. "Are you free now?"

"I'm free as I'll ever be." He held her hand and together, they sat on the ground. Lord moved her so she sat between his spread thighs. He held his palms up and she pressed hers down on his. Her hands were so much smaller than his.

He pressed his face against her neck, breathing her in, wanting to consume all of her.

This world was not meant for the likes of Ally. She was too good for them.

"I could stay here all day."

Letting go of her hands, he wrapped his arms around her waist. "Yeah?"

"Yeah. The sun is out. Do you think we should set up the grill? The guys could use some happiness. They're all frowning. The girls don't look happy either."

Lord glanced over her shoulder and he saw a couple of the guys were drinking coffee, talking, but the tension in their bodies was clear for him to read. They were ready for an attack, as was he. He just controlled himself better.

"You see them, don't you?"

"I see it all. It's not like I'm someone important, so they don't hide it from me. I get it. They're scared about something or someone. I'm not sure what it is yet, but I'll find out." She tilted her head back to look at him. "You're like that sometimes as well."

"I am?" he asked.

"Yes. I saw you this morning as we woke up. The first thing you did was go to the window and look out. You're waiting for something."

He pressed a kiss to her neck. "We're not scared, Ally. Don't mistake that emotion. We're used to people wanting what we've got. That doesn't make us scared. It makes us ready." He pulled back and ran a hand through his hair. "I want to take you to a safe place."

This had her turning in his arms. "What?"

"You heard. This compound, it's going to become

a war zone."

"And? I thought you said it always was."

He couldn't stand to see the pain in her eyes. Ally was so different to the women he was used to. Her sweetness fucking killed him. He had to do something to protect it though. "This is different. The Skull Nation are not the same as other enemies. They have numbers."

"That you can beat. You've told me they're nothing."

He cupped her face and forced her to look at him. "The Skull Nation are nothing to me unless I've got someone who is important to me. They know my weakness and I can't have that, Ally. They cannot know what you mean to me." He ran his thumb across her bottom lip. "I can't bear to lose you."

Tears swam in her eyes, but rather than let them affect him, he ignored them. "You said I'm safest by your side. Now, you're going to send me away?"

"Yes. I've got a safe house. It's not too far from here. It's a ranch. I know the handler. He's a good man. Strong. He was a brother until he left the club to help his wife and kids. Ranching life called to him."

She shook her head. "Look what happened last time. They found me at the hotel. I don't want to leave you."

"It won't be permanent. Just until I've got everything together." He pulled her close and kissed her hard on the mouth. His cock hardened but for now, he had to keep his mind in check. All it would take was one touch, to watch or feel her come around his cock, and he'd give in.

She was an addiction he didn't want to get rid of but for her own safety, he was going to do it.

"I want you to go and pack a bag. We leave immediately," he said.

He stood up and helped her to her feet. Without another look in her direction, he made his way into his office and picked up his phone.

It was a number he memorized but never thought he'd call.

"Well, well, well, I never thought I'd get a call from you," Rancher said.

Lord rubbed at his eyes. "And I never thought I'd call you."

"I'm guessing this is urgent business."

"It is." He was silent as he weighed up his options. Calling Rancher was a last resort.

"Lord, brother, what is it?" Rancher asked.

"I've got a girl."

"Club pussy?"

His hands clenched. "No."

"Wow, who knew with one word you could sound as possessive as fuck. She's not club?"

"She's mine."

"Okay. What do you need?"

He breathed deeply. What the fuck did he need? First, a brand-new set of balls. Second, to not be falling for the woman who was only supposed to be a toy to him. He rubbed at his temples but still, he wasn't happy about what he was doing. Ally didn't deserve this. The thought of Skull Nation getting to her, well, that settled it.

"I need a safe house for her."

"You want to bring her here?"

"Yes. I know you can protect her." Rancher had once been his VP. Brick a close second until Rancher had fallen deeply in love with his own sweet woman. "If your woman will allow her."

"Fuck, man. You know Betty isn't the one who wanted me to quit the club. It was a decision I made. No one else. My wife supported me in the club."

He still left though.

For Lord, it was never an option.

The club was in his blood. It was who he was and there was no getting away from that.

"Do I need to know what kind of danger you're in?" Rancher asked.

"The Skull Nation."

"Those bunch of pussies aren't worth your time, Lord."

"They weren't. Now they're making themselves known. They're causing me trouble and you know I don't like it when someone does that."

"Yeah, you get pissy when they do. Should I be worried?"

"I've got it handled. They'll come for me. Not for you. Hide her for me. Keep her safe."

"She's not one of these chicks that moans, is she?"

Lord laughed. "No."

"Damn, part of me was hoping you'd say yes so I knew your ass was in trouble." Rancher laughed. "Bring her now. I'll get everything set up."

"Thank you."

"Don't worry about it. I owe you one, remember."

Once men were initiated into the life, no one could leave. Rancher was more than just a club brother, he was a friend. During their time together, Rancher had taken more than his share of bullets. Lord didn't see it as being indebted to him.

Rancher earned his right to leave, and he'd granted it without a second thought. He looked toward the door to see Ally with a single bag packed.

Her eyes were red, but she wasn't crying now.

"I can help you here," she said. "Please, Lord. We belong together."

"I know what I'm doing, Ally. I've got to do everything in my power to protect you." He grabbed his car keys. There was no way he was risking his bike. He took the case from her and headed out of the clubhouse. Brick was entering as he left. Lord gave him a quick update before heading out to his car.

After throwing her case in the back, he climbed behind the wheel, waiting. In a matter of seconds, Brick and a couple of other brothers were out, straddling their bikes, ready to go with him.

Lord was tempted to order them back inside, but if for whatever reason The Skull Nation decided to attack, he wanted the numbers.

Turning over his ignition, he made his way out of the clubhouse, heading down the road, toward the ranch. It wasn't too close. There was a good distance and silence filled the car.

"Are you going to ignore me the whole way?" he asked.

"I don't have anything to say to you."

"It's for your own good."

"According to you," she said. "Last time, you brought me with you. You said it's safer if I go wherever you go. I don't understand."

"Ally, I know you're angry."

"You're sending me away to protect me, but who's going to protect *you*?"

He gritted his teeth. "I've got an entire clubhouse to protect me." He heard her snort. "Ally?"

"An entire clubhouse to protect you and yet you're sending me away. It tells me that for as much as you trust them, you don't think they've got what it takes to help me."

"I'm their leader, Ally. You're not."

"I'm just the woman you decided to keep for your own entertainment. Don't worry, Lord. I know my place."

This wasn't what he wanted to talk about. She was more than just a plaything. He knew that and he bet most of The Skull Nation knew that as well. Rather than argue with her, he remained silent for the rest of the journey.

He turned down a dirt road, going in the direction of Rancher's. Several cars were parked in the driveway and the man himself was already waiting.

Without a word to Ally, he parked the car, climbed out, and grabbed her case. Rancher was already walking toward him, holding out a hand, which he shook. "I didn't think I'd care for your ugly-ass face, but damn it is good to see you."

Ally climbed out of the car.

"Wow," Rancher said.

"Please, take care of her." He handed the case to Rancher as Ally joined them. Without another backward glance, he climbed into the car, and left the ranch, knowing he'd made the best decision he could. He couldn't let Ally go, but for now, he could at least keep her somewhere, he knew she was safe.

****

The following day, Ally made herself useful by helping Betty with the daily chores, which included laundry, cleaning, and cooking. Rancher didn't work alone. He had a small workforce. All of which Betty cooked for, including their three kids. Ally tended to the vegetable garden.

Betty talked nonstop all day and Ally enjoyed the distraction, but for now, she wanted peace and quiet to be able to reflect on the past twenty-four hours. She wasn't in the best of moods, that was for sure.

She'd known embarrassment and humiliation her entire life because of her father. The way Lord had treated her yesterday, well, she had no doubt he wanted to be rid of her. He hadn't kissed her goodbye. He hadn't said anything to her. She was nothing but a hindrance.

"I don't know what my runner beans have done to upset you, but if you're not careful, you'll ruin the entire crop," Rancher said, pulling her from her thoughts.

She didn't even realize she'd been brutalizing the tree before he started to talk. "I'm so sorry. I didn't mean to do that."

"Don't worry about it. Runner beans are quite resilient."

He perched against a small wall that enclosed the garden.

"I was only trying to help."

"And stay out of Betty's way. She said so."

"Oh, I didn't mean it like that," she said.

He chuckled and held up his hand. She noticed his arms were covered with ink and some peeked out beneath the collar of his shirt.

"My wife knows she can talk better than anyone. I swear she could have been a lawyer. The woman knows how to keep on talking."

"She's really nice."

"And sometimes you need to escape to be able to think," he said.

"I hope I haven't upset her."

Rancher shook his head. "It's impossible to upset her." The smile on his lips as he thought about his wife made Ally slightly envious. He clearly loved her.

"I never said thank you yesterday. For taking me in and for the lovely room. The food. All of it."

"It's not every day Lord calls. In fact, this is the

first time since I left the club that he ever has."

She glanced down at the bucket of runner beans. "I don't mean to be trouble."

"You're not the trouble, Ally. Those assholes that want to take out the club would hurt you."

"He didn't move out any of the other women," she said.

"That's because they don't matter. Half of the women are there for the easy life. All they've got to do is give up their bodies to the men, and they don't have to do anything."

"Apart from what they're told," she said.

"Again, not a bad life considering the alternative. The women know the score there. They're not victims. They seek out the club, not the other way around."

"I didn't seek out the club. I was taken. Lord was supposed to kill me." She squeezed her hands together. "I don't know if I was supposed to tell you that."

"Instead, Lord fell for you?"

"Lord didn't fall for me. I'm..." Her cheeks started to heat. There was no way she could tell this stranger what uses Lord had for her.

"I can imagine what my good friend would say and do to get what he wanted," Rancher said. "Lord's rough around the edges. There was a time I didn't think he had a heart, then I was proven otherwise."

"How?"

"I'm here. Alive and well. Living a life I never thought possible. I'm here because of him. You're here because of him."

"You don't have to sing his praises." The last thing she wanted to hear right now was how good Lord could be. She wanted to hate him. It would be a lot easier if she did. Even when he said he couldn't get rid of her, he had.

"You love him?"

She looked up at Rancher. "I don't know what I feel."

"I'm guessing you hate him a great deal right now."

"I don't want to talk about it." She picked some more runner beans and decided she'd ruined that plant enough for now, and so she went to go and use some of the peas. Betty had given her a list of vegetables that were needed for the next couple of days. Being out in the garden wasn't something she considered fun, but it beat being in the house missing Lord. At least outside, she could pretend to live a normal life.

"He's a hard man to love."

"It's just an arrangement," she said.

"You're pissed at him?"

She snapped off a few pods and threw them into the basket with the other beans. "You really want to talk to me?"

"I consider Lord a good friend. I worry about him."

"Then why don't you go and help him? I know this stuff with the Skull Nation is getting to him." Even as she wanted to hate Lord, she couldn't help but be worried about him. Who wouldn't be? The life he led brought nothing but danger.

There was no way she could help him. She hadn't been able to help herself.

"It's not my place. I just don't want you thinking bad of him. He's doing this for your own good and what's more, the fact you're the only one he moved speaks volumes."

She stared at him for several seconds but didn't say a word.

"I'll let you get back to your picking." He nodded

at her and then left the garden. Alone with her thoughts, she blew out a breath.

Snapping each new pea pod, she filled her bucket and then carried them into the kitchen where Betty waited with a sink full of water.

Tipping the food into the sink, she sank her hands in and started to wash them. She placed them on the clean drainer and waited to see how Betty handled them.

"Are you okay?"

"Yeah, I'm fine. Did you send your husband to talk to me?"

"Nah. Rancher has a tendency to do whatever the hell he wants. I didn't ask for him to quit the club the way he did. He just wanted to start a fresh life for me. I was pregnant at the time and they'd just had an attack on the compound. It shook him up."

Ally paused. "Really?"

"The clubhouse gets attacked. Not all fights are at businesses. It was a long day because after the attack, I got these pains. I'd never felt them before. The doctor put me on bed rest. I nearly lost the baby. Rancher blamed himself, of course. To him, you can't have the club and kids."

Ally wiped at her forehead.

"I never wanted him to leave as I know there are times he worries, even now. At least we're able to do his for him. Lord is a good man." Betty frowned and laughed. "I know it's really hard for me to say that in one sentence, but he is. Don't get on his bad side. Then you're in real trouble. The club will always hold his loyalty."

Ally took a deep breath. "Why are you and Rancher doing this? I'm not going to leave Lord."

"I know it can be challenging, falling for a hard man. There is always goodness in them."

She thought back to what she witnessed within the first twenty-four hours of being in Lord's company. He'd killed a man, threatened her life, and then gave her a chance to earn her freedom.

Do you even want to be free?

Having sex with someone for the first time didn't mean anything. Women gave up their virginity all the time.

"I've upset you?" Betty asked.

"No. I'm … worried. I haven't heard from him today. I know he only dropped me off yesterday, but I'm still concerned."

What if the Skull Nation attacked the clubhouse? Lord could be dying right this second and she wouldn't know.

"Do you think I could call him? Talk to him?" she asked.

"Sure. We've got his number." Betty wiped her hands on a towel and disappeared. Ally finished washing the last of the beans, followed by the pea pods when Betty returned. She had a phone in one hand and a number in the other. "We've never used this number. I don't know if it's working. Rancher would be the best one to tell you, but you could try it."

She took the cell phone and the number. "Thank you. Do you mind if I … go?"

"Of course. Go right ahead. I'll still be working on these when you're done." Betty smiled.

Ally made her way to the spare bedroom.

Calling Lord, was it desperate? She missed him and the clubhouse. Even with all the people who couldn't stand her.

She typed the number into the phone and waited for a second before pressing the button to activate the call.

Chapter Ten

They'd gotten a few leads. Lord knew where the Skull Nation VP was hiding out. The other club had spread out, trying to remain untouchable, invisible. They didn't know how capable the Straight to Hell MC really were. Once Lord got his hands on the VP, he'd torture him, make an example of the fucker. He'd let him call for backup, then the real party would get started.

Their businesses up north had been cleaned up and he had extra men patrolling to ensure their enemies didn't try to infiltrate again. Lord wasn't ready to hand over one of his cash cows on a silver platter. He'd die before he let his enemies get the better of his club.

Tank and Tarmac had been making bullets on their presses for the past few days straight. They were ready for Armageddon. The amount of lead they'd stockpiled was impressive. The boys were getting ready. They were riding out after sunset.

Lord sat in his office. Alone. He didn't want anyone near him now. He needed to stay focused on tonight, but it was next to impossible when he kept thinking of Ally. She was supposed to be temporary, not take over his whole world. No one had to tell him, even though he'd never experienced it before … he was falling in love. And his love was unlike any other man's. It was deep and dark, had a life of its own. Just thinking of her made his entire body come alive. His heart would beat faster and his gray mood would improve.

He was thinking of stupid bullshit that he had no right to be thinking. What would happen to her if he got killed? Who'd take care of her?

No one had ever put him first. His childhood was a shitstorm that started his road into trouble and crime. But now Ally had become his everything. He lived and breathed for that slip of a girl and there was nothing he could do to backtrack his feelings now.

His cell went off. Lord leaned back in his office chair, the hinge giving a slight squeak. It was an old number he vaguely remembered. One he'd given to Rancher a long time ago. Why would he call from that number and not his new one?

Was there trouble?

He sat up straight, bringing the phone to his ear. "Rancher?"

The line was dead.

He tensed, his jaw twitching. A hundred horrific scenarios played in his head.

Rather than drive himself crazy, he dialed back the number.

It kept ringing, stirring his anxiety into overdrive. "Hello?"

It was *her* voice. The perfect, musical voice of his little virgin. She was alive.

"Are you okay?"

Silence.

"Ally? Answer me now."

"I'm sorry for calling. I know it's only been a day. I'm sorry," she said.

"Why'd you hang up?"

"I didn't want you to think I was being clingy. I don't want to push you away more because it seems I'm already very good at that."

"You're not pushing me away, baby. I'm just keeping you safe. But, trust me, I haven't stopped thinking of you."

"Really?" More silence. "When will I see you again? I keep thinking something horrible is happening. I hate being here not knowing anything."

"Soon."

"I need you, Lord."

The yearning in her voice only mirrored how he felt. How was he supposed to focus tonight with his mind on Ally and his cock hard for her?

He didn't think long. "I'll be there in twenty minutes," he said. "Meet me in the lane behind the barn. Wear a skirt with no panties."

He hung up the phone and mentally kicked himself. This had to be his secret or the boys would call him pussy-whipped. He felt like a love-sick teenager, but there was no doubt he had to see Ally. Last night, in bed alone, he'd had too much time with his own thoughts. He needed her by his side. She was healing. Innocent. She chased away his demons without even realizing it.

Now he'd promised himself as much as her that they'd be together within the hour. No backing out now. He was an idiot, always taking risks to be with Ally.

Lord headed out to his bike. The sky was clear, the sun reflecting off the chrome. This would be a short and sweet trip. He'd be back long before they had to get ready for tonight. Seeing her would give him enough peace until he had her back at the club again.

He kicked his bike to life, the purr stirring his body. Reaper approached him before he could escape unseen. "You need someone to ride with you?"

"Not this time. I won't be long."

His enforcer raised a brow. "You're seeing her, aren't you?"

He revved his engine. "Rally the men as we planned. I'll be back in time." Then he rode off without further explanation.

He didn't understand why Rancher would leave the club. Lord didn't understand love. Couldn't understand sacrificing everything for one woman.

Now he knew exactly what his old friend had

gone through.

He craved the same thing with Ally, only he couldn't give up his club. Lord needed to find a balance between the two, and the biggest obstacle would be keeping Ally safe. In his world, enemies sought out weaknesses. The greatest target was a loved one. They could be used against you, make you weak. Lord had done the same thing for many of his enemies. Ally was in his life for this reason alone. He wanted to make her father suffer, to exact revenge for his lack of loyalty. Now he had to protect her from men just like himself.

The lane was unpaved, so he slowed down his bike as he neared Rancher's back gate. Just the anticipation of seeing Ally make his cock stir in his jeans.

He hoped she was there waiting for him.

He needed her.

There were overgrown trees in the way, so he couldn't see if she was near the gate. As he pulled closer, he noticed her outline in the shadow of a new outbuilding that hadn't been there before.

He parked next to the shed and cut his engine.

It had only been twenty-four hours. He shouldn't crave her this much. It felt like she'd been away from him for weeks or months, not hours.

Lord braced an arm on the low split rail fence and hopped over. He approached her, slowly, cautiously.

"You came."

"It's okay, Ally. I wasn't stupid enough to come straight here. I wasn't followed."

"That's not what I mean."

He cupped her face and kissed her. It felt like their first kiss all over again—deep and addicting. She tasted sweet and he wanted more.

"I couldn't keep away," he whispered against her

lips.

"Good."

He wrapped an arm around her, pulling her flush to his body. Her soft curves pressed against his hardness.

"They treating you right here?" he asked

She nodded, toying with the buttons on his cut.

"You behaving yourself? Keeping safe?"

"I want to come home," she said.

His insecurities must run deep. "Where's home?"

She scowled, a look of confusion on her face. "With you. At the club."

He exhaled. That was exactly what he wanted to hear. When she used to talk about leaving or returning to her old life, it made him anxious because he couldn't lose her. He was keeping her regardless, but knowing it was her choice to stay was the ultimate high.

"I want you there too. Tonight, we're riding out, cleaning up some shit."

"Will it be dangerous?"

"Don't worry about me, Ally. I'm invincible, remember?"

"You're not." She ran her fingertips along the scar beside his blind eye. Normally, a touch like that would make him see red. She broke down all his barriers.

He kissed her hard on the mouth, walking her backward until she was pinned to the new shed. Lord raked his fingers into the hair behind her neck, holding her in place as they kissed. With his free hand, he reached low between them to see if she'd followed his instructions.

Her pussy was nice and smooth, no panties in his way. He impaled two fingers hard into her cunt and she gasped into his mouth. "Do you like that?" His words sounded rough, like a man on the edge. He felt like a fucking man out of prison for the first time in twenty years.

"Yes." She breathed the words, barely above a whisper. "I want you inside me."

Ally was playing with fire. She had no idea how pent-up he felt.

He unbuckled and attempted to get his jeans open, but her little hands were there trying to help, hindering his progress. By the time he released his cock, he groaned with relief. She wrapped her hand possessively around his length.

Lord grabbed her wrist to stop her. "I'm too far gone for that, baby." He hoisted her up against the building, immediately seeking out her entrance. She was wet, so he easily impaled her to the hilt. She cried out, squeezing his shoulders, and he rammed into her hard and fast. Her tight little pussy felt like heaven wrapped around his dick.

"Oh, God, Lord. That feels so good."

"You're all mine, Ally. Mine to fuck. Mine to keep."

"Yes, I'm yours." She wrapped her arms around his neck as he began to thrust inside her. He felt whole having her in his grasp.

"Take it all, baby." He fucked her deep, holding each thigh just under her ass.

"Give it to me."

****

Each time Lord thrust inside her, he rubbed against her clit. Over and over, the stimulation had her close to orgasm. As she'd waited alone near the back gate, the drone of crickets her only company, her mind had been a whirlwind of thoughts and desires. She could already feel him, smell him, and once she saw him ride up on his Harley, her pussy throbbed in anticipation.

He was her everything.

Once her captor, now her only love.

His big, hard body made her feel safe. The scent of his cologne mixed with the leather of his cut was unique to him. As their bodies molded together, his cock connecting them intimately, she felt whole. She didn't want to live a life without Lord. Looking back, she wasn't even sure how she managed.

He took care of her, made her feel beautiful and wanted.

Right now, even though he wasn't taking his time, it still felt like they were making love. Every time they kissed, she always felt a unique passion between them. The entire world went away and it was just the two of them.

He kissed her as he fucked her, his tongue claiming her mouth. Lord devoured her, body and soul. His rough stubble scraped her face, his big hands squeezing her ass as he supported most of her weight.

"I need you, Lord."

Her breathing became labored. She was so close to coming but tried to hold off. She wanted this day to last forever. Nothing was ever guaranteed in his world.

"Come for me, Ally. Come now!"

His growled words and forceful tone brought her over that edge, and she couldn't hold off for another second. She allowed herself to embrace her orgasm, waves of heat and energy racing through her core.

Lord rammed into her, the entire shed buckling. With his final groan, he filled her with his seed, his cock throbbing on and on.

He exhaled, his shoulders briefly resting against her. "I haven't stopped thinking of you since I dropped you off yesterday. It killed me to leave you behind. The bedroom was too quiet, too lonely without you beside me in bed."

Every word he spoke was music to her ears. After what Rancher and Betty had told her, she should believe that Lord loved her. All the signs pointed to it. But she still had doubts and nagging insecurities. Hearing the truth from Lord's own mouth made her feel complete, wanted.

"Same here. I cried myself to sleep last night. I felt like you just wanted me gone. I'm the only one you sent away."

"Because you're the only one who matters." He lowered her down to her feet and buttoned his jeans.

"Are you leaving again?" She knew the answer but didn't want to believe it. There was always that hope inside her.

"We have to ride out tonight. I just needed to see you before then."

She wrapped her arms around his waist and rested her head against his chest. He stroked her hair. It felt so good that she closed her eyes, trying to hear his heartbeat. It was too tempting to tell him everything on her mind.

"What if something happens to you?" she whispered.

"I've been thinking about it. A lot. If something happens to me, I want you taken care of, Ally. I'm going to tell Locke to make sure you're set up financially."

She shook her head, pulling away, but he held her arms, keeping her in place. "It was just a hypothetical question, Lord. The way you're talking is like you expect it to happen. You think they'll kill you tonight, don't you?"

"I'm just being smart. I'm not afraid of dying, but knowing you'd be left to fend for yourself is too much for me to bear."

"No, no! I don't want any money. I don't want to

be set up somewhere. What I want is you. Us. A *family*."

She kept quiet after, realizing how loud she'd been. Realizing *what* she'd said.

It was all true though. As crazy as it sounded, she wanted a family with her MC prez. It wouldn't be typical, but they'd make it perfect.

"Ally, please."

"Can't you send them and stay behind? You're the boss. They have to listen to you." Tears began to prick her eyes and a frog burned in her throat. "Please, Lord."

"Oh, baby." He pulled her close, even though she fought him. He kissed the top of her head. "Please don't do this to me. You know I have to go."

"You don't!"

"We all ride after sunset. Nothing will happen to me. Everything will happen to the asshole we're after. We're well-armed, prepared, and trained for this. You can't worry every time I have to clean up shit. If you're going to be my old lady, you have to be able to handle your emotions, Ally."

She swallowed hard. "You haven't talked about that for a while."

"Well, I think about it often," he said. "When this is over and you're back at the club, I'm going to make it official."

Her heart felt as if it would burst. She knew the magnitude of what he was saying. It was what she most wanted.

"Promise?"

He smiled down at her. For such a hard ass, he had the most beautiful smile. There was a dimple there, too.

"I should go." He stroked her hair. The adoration in his eyes was impossible to dismiss. He was being genuine. She wondered if he'd ever tell her he loved her and mean it. Ally would take what she could get, and being named his old lady said a lot.

"You only just got here."

"You think I want Rancher knowing I was here? He'll never let me forget it. I have a reputation to upkeep." He winked at her.

"Lord, you better come back to us or I'll kill you."

"Yes, ma'am."

He began walking backward. She admired his muscular frame, wanting to keep him in her bed for a week straight. Not wanting him to leave and risk his life.

She knew bits and pieces of his past, his childhood, and all the scars. He deserved a happily ever after, even if it was an unorthodox one. If he died in a club war, who would remember him? Maybe only her.

Not even their child would know who he was. Only what she told him. Or *her*.

Every cell in her body fired off to spill the truth, but she resisted the instinct to run after him. Ally was pregnant. She'd found out late last night. There were several unused pregnancy tests in the bathroom cupboard. With their love of kids, she wouldn't be surprised if Betty and Rancher were actively trying for another one.

Ally couldn't burden Lord with this revelation before he rode out. He needed a clear and level head in order to stay safe and come back to her. And she wouldn't use the baby to blackmail him into staying behind tonight.

When she told him about the baby, it would be once they were together, their world not in chaos.

"I'll be back soon," he said before hopping over the fence. "Behave yourself."

She nodded.

As soon as the bike engine fired to life, her emotions bubbled up. She put on a happy face, fighting away the tears. The sound meant he was leaving. She already knew the loneliness and dread she'd feel once he was too far for her to hear that roar.

No matter how great Rancher and Betty treated her, this was their home, their life. She felt like an outsider because she was. What she needed was the club, which was the last thing she'd expect to want in her life.

"Please come back to us," she whispered to herself.

Ally held her stomach, not knowing if she could face a pregnancy alone. She didn't want to be a single mother. If Lord died, she doubted his men would respect his wishes to look out for her. She'd be on her own.

He rode off alone and her tears began to flow.

Part of her knew it would be the last time she ever saw him again.

Chapter Eleven

The motel where the Skull Nation VP was hanging out was a pile of crap. Lord looked at the place and truly believed it was crawling with termites or some shit. He'd seen four rats as they scurried across the street, clearly not caring if they were seen or not. He hated vermin so much.

His boys stood at his back, ready to do whatever he asked.

They'd left their bikes a few miles down the road.

"Holy shit, I didn't think I had standards," Brick said.

"Me too, but I wouldn't stay in this shit hole."

"Anyone think the VP is getting desperate?" Reaper asked.

Tarmac let out a shudder. "Guys, we've got to go in that place."

"You think there's more than one of the assholes in there?" Brick asked.

"No, I guessing the VP is in there alone. They've spread out, trying to gain ground by splitting down their group." It was a trick Lord had done a few times but he'd learned fast from his mistake. What the Skull Nation had done had split them down too far and too wide.

There was no sense in splitting up to only a singular person. All it did was make it a lot easier for enemies to take you out one by one.

He hadn't lost men for the decision to split like that up, but it had been close. They'd been hurt badly and had taken months to recover. This was years ago. Now he knew there was safety in numbers. Like now.

"I don't like this," Brick said.

Rather than roll out the entire club, Lord had kept a selection of men back at the clubhouse, while he'd taken the other few to the motel. This way, if the Skull Nation MC planned to take over his clubhouse, they were in for a rude awakening. There were two prospects on the lookout while the others were loaded up, ready to take them on. No one would get through his walls.

His club was sticking together. They had their weapons at the ready and he was done waiting around, staring at a parking lot with a couple of cars spread out here or there.

He stepped forward, pulling his gun out of his back waistband. As he advanced toward the enemy, his thoughts returned to Ally. Brick had caught him returning. Neither of them had spoken, but his VP knew where he'd been.

Ally was the woman he didn't want to give up.

He loved her. He couldn't deny it.

She'd started out as a plaything, and he'd been addicted to her virginity, but it had soon advanced from there.

He wanted to keep her. There was no way he could be without her.

With his men at his back, he took the stairs leading him to the third floor. He slowed down so as not to alert the VP they were coming.

Once he stood in front of the door, Brick took the left, Reaper took the right. The rest of the men were tense and ready.

One.

Two.

Three.

He slammed his booted foot against the door and it flew open, crashing back as a woman screamed. Storming into the room, he caught sight of the naked woman scrambling to get off the man.

Her fake tits barely moved and the man himself

was none other than the VP, who reached for his gun next to the pillow.

Lord fired and the man screamed as the bullet went straight through his hand.

The woman quickly wrapped a blanket around her. Her entire body was shaking. He caught sight of her clothes, and he grabbed them, throwing them at her.

"Get out," Lord said.

The woman rushed toward him, taking her stuff, and then glanced back, biting her lip.

Lord pressed his gun to her head. "Do you want me to kill you?"

"He hasn't paid me. Please, I don't want to die. I've got children to support."

Lord saw the man's wallet, went to it, took out all the cash, and handed it to her.

She scampered out of the way.

He heard the unmistakable sound of one of his men slapping her ass as she left, along with her answer to call her.

This was why he didn't think he'd ever be able to love a woman. But Ally was nothing like them. She'd entered his world and completely obliterated his idea of what he thought a woman should be like.

The VP sat on the bed and laughed. "You found me." Perspiration dotted his brow.

Lord stared at him, not impressed by what he saw.

All he could think about was killing him. It would be easy. A single bullet to the head. It was what he knew. Between the cold, clean kill and the way the Skull Nation had pissed him off, he was ready to take them out, one by fucking one. He'd be happy to allow the streets to run red with blood. Relished the idea in fact.

Causing death didn't upset him. He reveled in it.

Counting in his mind, he stared at the heavily inked man. The Skull Nation was a fucking menace. A disease. Toxic. No one would miss them from this world.

"Prez?" Brick asked.

The man on the bed started to laugh. "Have cold feet, Lord?"

"Where's your prez?" he asked.

"As if I'm going to tell you."

Lord took aim and fired. This time, the bullet went through the man's arm. He fell back on the bed and screamed, blood splattered all over the white duvet.

He waited.

"Where is he?" Lord asked.

The man spat on the floor, sitting back up. "You think I'll tell you?"

Another shot fired, this time in the man's foot.

More howls of pain.

Lord was bored with this. He wanted this over with the Skull Nation. He didn't believe for a second it would be over completely. Wherever there was a Skull Nation, there would be trouble. Wiping out the men at the top would stop them from coming after him.

He wasn't willing to risk wiping out the entire club. It was a known fact another would take its place. While the Skull nation rebuilt, he'd be watching. He'd rather have a piece-of-shit club he knew than one he didn't that could take him on and kill him.

"You know I could do this all day," Lord said. "You're not going to get out of this alive."

The VP groaned. "I'm not a rat."

Another shot, this time, he went hardcore and for the abdomen.

The son of a bitch screamed even louder.

Lord waited.

He had all night.

There was no rush for him.

He watched the blood as it spread out on the bed. His men stayed perfectly still. Three of them had their guns trained on the VP in front of them. The rest were outside keeping an eye out.

No one would call the cops. In this neighborhood, the sound of a gunshot meant to stay indoors and not get involved.

In the back of his mind, he kept thinking about Ally.

Her sweetness and goodness.

She deserved better than him.

I'm not giving her up.

He couldn't give her up even if he wanted to. Bringing himself back into focus, he stared at the man and suddenly felt an overwhelming anger.

Lord put the safety on his gun and shoved it into the back of his jeans as he moved toward the VP. Grabbing him by his hair, he began to pull him off the bed.

The longer this lasted with the VP and chasing after random members of the Skull Nation, the longer he was parted from the love of his life.

Earlier, being inside her, that was heaven.

The night before, being away from her, was hell.

He had to get this shit sorted so he could move on.

The man screamed, trying to hit out at him. Lord stopped, landing a blow to his face.

"Get off me," the VP said.

"Lord?" Brick asked.

He ignored him. Lord used the man's head and smashed it through the window. Picking up a shard of glass, he began to impale it piece by piece into the VP, being very careful not to get any major veins.

The man gasped as Lord went toward his dick.

"Stop. Stop."

Lord stared at the man. "We could have done this the easy way."

The man whimpered. "You call this the fucking easy way?"

Lord ran the edge of the piece of glass along the man's dick.

"Fuck, no, fuck." He began to cough. "You want to know where the prez is?" the man asked.

"That was my question. I wouldn't still be here with you. Admittedly, you'd be dead, but it wouldn't hurt quite this bad." He pressed down on a piece of embedded glass, and the man screamed.

He let go, giving him a few seconds to gain his composure. "I'm waiting, and I've always wanted to sever a dick this way." He had no intention of touching that infected thing. It looked disgusting.

The VP coughed and laughed. "I did my job."

"Excuse me?" Lord asked as a shiver ran down his spine.

"Where do you think he is?" The VP laughed. "All he needed was some additional time." The man spat at him. "I'm already dying, you fucking prick. I've got less than three months to live. I was just helping my prez out. She's really a hot piece of ass, your girl. He simply wanted what you have. You should have known not to leave her alone."

****

"I honestly don't know how you do it," Ally said, smiling at Betty as she came downstairs. She'd put her children to bed a while ago.

Rancher had been out in the fields mending some fences with some of his ranch hands earlier. Now he was checking on his animals before bed.

"What? Help run a ranch, feed my children and men, clean, attend a garden, and still have time to do a little reading?"

"You're like … wow." Ally laughed. "I'm exhausted watching you."

"That happens in the first trimester."

Ally stopped smiling. "You know?"

Betty took a seat beside her. "Rancher came into the bedroom last night and asked if we'd made another one. We're trying. We love having kids and well, I love Rancher. I told him it wasn't mine and seeing as the only other fertile woman on the ranch is you, we deduced it had to be."

"I threw it in the trash," Ally said. "I didn't leave it lying around."

Betty laughed and put a hand on her arm. "Please, don't worry about it. My husband is a pain in the ass. I know him well, and he probably went into the trash to see what it was."

"Have you been trying long?" Ally asked.

"A couple of months." Betty shrugged. "I'm not worried. I'm of the mindset that what will be, will be. You know? I don't see a reason to worry. If I'm supposed to have babies, I will. If I'm not, I won't. Simple as that."

"You're very … philosophical."

"Someone would say philosophical. Another would say I refuse to allow what's not happening in my life to wear me down. Rancher and I, we'll work it out."

Ally put a hand on her own stomach.

Would she and Lord work it out?

"Does Lord know?" Betty asked.

She nibbled on her lip and shook her head. "No, I didn't have time to tell him."

"Even earlier?"

Ally quickly looked toward Betty who chuckled. "Yes, we saw you sneaking out of the house. Rancher thought you were meeting some guy. Maybe one of the enemies. He kept an eye on you and I told him Lord was coming."

"Rancher thought I'd betray Lord?"

"It's not personal. He doesn't know you. He'd protecting his friend. Lord and Rancher haven't seen much of each other in recent years, but when they're together, it doesn't matter. That's true friendship, and I never want to come between that."

"I would never hurt Lord."

Betty rubbed her arm. "I know that. When we saw Lord, Rancher felt bad. Don't worry, I made Rancher feel good."

Ally sighed. "I missed him."

"I figured."

"Do you really think he could love me, though? A man like Lord. You've seen me and I've seen the women hanging out at the club."

Betty held her hand up and shook her head. "I'm going to stop you right there."

"But—"

"No. You don't get to talk like that. You think I don't know what it's like? To know your husband is hanging around with skanks."

"I don't imagine they're all skanks."

Betty laughed. "And you wonder why Lord wants you. You're different. He's used to women throwing themselves at every single guy with a dick. All of the women. They can't seem to say no to a cock. If you're been around the club long enough, you'll see it. You'll know it. They're looking to make a name for themselves. Some of the women want long-term. They want an easy life that the men provide. Others want the reputation of screwing every man in the club. They're patch whores. The more men they fuck, the more valued they think they are. I know it doesn't make sense. Believe me, I don't get it. But to them, it does." Betty sighed. "You can't let them get to you. They're like vultures. If they spot any weakness at all in you, that's it. It's all over."

Ally sighed. "I really need to tell him. Don't I?"

"Yeah, you really do. Lord is a good man. He told me to take care of his boy and that's all I've been doing." Betty looked ahead. "I didn't imagine for a second we'd be where we're at today. I love him so much. I adore the life we've built, but we did it together. Talk to Lord. He wants you."

"How can you be so sure?"

"He snuck onto our land to have his way with you. That guy is pussy whipped."

There was a sudden whimper.

"That's my call. I'll be back. Think about it." Betty patted her knee and then got up.

Ally watched her go.

Leaning back on the sofa, she put her hands on her stomach. "Did you hear that? Lord is pussy whipped. Your daddy wants me. Well, I hope he does. Either way, I'm going to love you enough."

Her nerves were getting the better of her.

She rubbed her stomach, wondering when she'd really start to show. The sudden urge for some hot chocolate overcame her, and she got to her feet, making her way toward the kitchen.

Making herself at home inside their ranch was hard.

She grabbed two mugs from the cupboard before opening the fridge. She poured out two mugs of milk and then put it into the saucepan. Next, she had the pan on the stove, heating up.

She went through each cupboard, looking for some chocolate mix. The moment she found it, she smiled.

Score.

Just as she was sprinkling the powder into the milk, Ally paused as she heard the unmistakable sound of bikes entering the front yard.

Turning off the burner, she put the packet on the counter and rushed toward the front door. Her heart raced and she couldn't wipe the smile off her face.

Without looking, she opened it up and stepped onto the porch, only to come to a stop.

It was dark and the floodlight had turned on as the bikes arrived.

The insignia wasn't Lord's.

She recognized it as the Skull Nation MC.

Before she had a chance to react, Betty was there, already thinking ahead.

"Fuck. Shit. Fuck." Betty slammed the locks closed.

"Mommy?"

The bikes and lights must have woken the kids.

"Go and hide, baby. Do as I've told you. All of you. Go and hide. Now!"

Bullets rained down on the house, shattering glass.

Betty grabbed her hand, and together, they ran upstairs. She expected them to go to the children, but they ran to her bedroom.

Ally didn't know what the hell she was doing.

"Call Rancher."

"I don't have a cell phone."

"Open the fucking window and yell. He's in the barn. Just keep on yelling." Betty had pulled a box out from under the bed. It had a lock on it and she was

THE BIKER'S PLAYTHING

surprised how Betty was able to get into it. The woman's hands shook.

Rushing to the back window, she pushed it up and yelled Rancher's name at the top of her lungs. She did this over and over again until the sound of a door slamming open interrupted her.

Ally looked toward Betty.

Her gun was loaded, and she grabbed Ally's hand. They ran through to the bathroom. She closed the door and snapped the lock into place.

"What do we do?" Ally asked.

"We stay silent."

"What about the kids?"

Betty shook her head. "This is what Rancher's been training us for. They know what to do and they play the game how to stay quiet. They all have to be so silent that no one will ever know they're there. He's the one who adapted this house."

"Betty, they're the Skull Nation."

"I know."

"They're going to kill us." She'd never get to tell Lord she was pregnant. Holy crap, had she and Lord gotten Betty, Rancher, and their kids killed?

"Rancher will come. He always promised to protect me. He'll be here." Betty held the gun up and aimed at the door.

"But … what if he doesn't?" Ally asked.

Betty opened her mouth, closed it. "He won't let me down. He never has. I trust him. He's coming."

Ally covered her mouth with her hand as they heard the loud footsteps of the men coming up the old wooden stairs.

If Rancher came, would he be able to take on the men alone? She saw at least three, but there could have been more.

135

All she wanted was Lord.

She didn't have a gun and as the bathroom door slammed open, Betty fired.

Ally screamed as one of the men grabbed Betty and threw her hard against the wall. The gun she'd been holding dropped to the floor. As Betty tried to attack, struggling wildly, she got slapped in the mouth and Ally finally saw red.

She screamed, charging at the man. His jacket claimed him to be the President of the Skull Nation club.

Jumping on his back, she brought her arm across his neck, hoping her weight would do something to stop him.

He slammed her back against the wall, the impact winding her.

Within seconds, he had his hands wrapped around her neck as he smiled at her. "I knew I'd find you."

Chapter Twelve

Lord cut off the guy's dick, then nodded to Brick. As soon as he stepped away from the howling piece of shit, his VP put a bullet between his eyes.

"We ride out *now*," he said.

This was the reason he'd sent Ally to stay with Rancher. He didn't trust the Skull Nation to use her against him. Now he wasn't sure if the VP had been fucking with him or telling the truth. What if they'd found out where Ally was staying?

She'd begged him to keep her at the club, and he was starting to believe it may have been the best choice. At least his compound was heavily fortified and protected by armed men. Rancher's place may be off the grid, but it wasn't a fort, and there was only one man guarding it. Rancher was a tough son of a bitch, but he wasn't invincible.

It wasn't supposed to go down this way.

He was certain he'd made the best choice. There was no way the Skull Nation could have found out what he'd done with Ally. As far as they were concerned, she was at home waiting for him.

Should he head back to the club or to Rancher's place? Time was of the essence right now. They'd killed the VP, but Lord wanted their prez.

"Call Righteous. Find out if there's any trouble at the club. Let them know to be ready for trouble," said Lord.

He headed back out to his bike, swinging his leg over the seat. Before starting the engine, he looked to Tarmac, waiting for an answer.

"No trouble at home, boss."

Lord kicked his bike to life and had one destination in mind. Even if the VP had been screwing with his head, he'd feel better knowing Ally was safe. Maybe he'd change his mind and bring her back to the clubhouse for his peace of mind.

Only his headlights on the asphalt ahead cut the pitch darkness. There didn't even seem to be a moon tonight. They were far off, no signs of civilization for miles. He couldn't believe how unsettled he felt. For decades, he'd lived on a fine line of life and death. Nothing much gave him pause because he didn't give a shit about himself or anyone else.

Ally changed everything.

He wanted to wake up tomorrow because she made him want more out of life. That girl would become his old lady. They'd make a family together. Lord would make sure his kids were raised properly so they didn't turn out fucked-up like him as adults.

Lord took a breath as he rode, keeping up the punishing pace. He'd lived through countless disappointments, even came close to ending his own life on a few occasions. But he wouldn't be able to come back from losing Ally. You couldn't kiss the sunshine and return to the darkness unscathed. It would destroy him.

First, he'd kill every single Skull Nation and their families, but he probably wouldn't stop there. Her death would turn him into a devil. And he'd welcome a bullet when his rampage was over just to end the pain. The way his life had panned out, he almost expected fate to steal her away from him.

Fuck, that hotel had been far out. Was that their plan all along? Lead him away from his woman?

As much as he didn't want to announce Ally's location in case that VP had been blowing smoke up his ass, he had to be safe.

Lord slowed down and pulled into a lookout point

along the side of the highway. The other brothers joined him moments later.

Reaper walked up to his side. "What's the trouble? Your bike?"

He shook his head. "You heard what he said. I'm not going to pretend everything's good. I'm calling Rancher to be safe." After pulling out his cell, he dialed his old friend. He hated the fact he could have put the man and his family at risk. It had never been his intention.

The phone kept ringing. It was after midnight, so he was probably sleeping. Or dead. *Fuck!*

Lord pocketed the phone, his chest tight. He was forty years old, and this shit couldn't be good for his health. "Reaper, give the club a call. Ask a couple patches to ride out to Rancher's place. It ain't far. Tell them to do some recon, make sure everything's on the up and up until we get there."

"Will do."

He headed back on the road, feeling somewhat relieved knowing things would be handled until he got home.

They'd been driving close to an hour but everything was becoming familiar now. They were close to Rancher's place in the country. At least there was no fire in the sky. He wasn't sure what he expected next to Armageddon. The night was just as dark out here as on the road. Rancher owned hundreds of acres, a mix of forest and farmland. It felt calm, like any other evening.

Lord smiled to himself as they neared the ranch. That VP was just messing with his head. Lord would have done the same thing if he'd been close to death at the hands of his enemy.

He wasn't sure if he should let them sleep or wake the whole damn house just because he wanted to bring Ally home to the club. When he saw the faint light on in an upstairs window, he was glad for it. Someone was awake, so that meant he could steal his woman away without being a complete asshole. Maybe he'd claim her ass tonight. Make her his in every way. Just thinking about her aroused him. Imagining all those soft curves, warm and comfortable in bed, were calling his name. Sleep was starting to pull at him, but his determined focus and the cold night air kept him alert.

He slowed down and entered the winding front path to the house. No sign of the Straight to Hell MC. All must have checked out.

Reaper pulled up alongside him.

They all stopped their bikes within plenty of distance to not wake the entire house with the roar of their engines. "You called the club?"

"Yeah, they said they'd come do a round. That was a while ago."

His headlights reflected off something metallic. There was one bike in front of the house. Maybe it was Rancher's.

He turned off his Harley and walked toward the old farmhouse, his hand on the butt of the gun in his waistband. The dry grass crunched under each footfall. The light in the window went black. His hackles began to rise, and he sure as hell hoped his intuition was wrong.

There was another bike. Neither were from his club. He didn't like this one fucking bit.

He nodded to his men to flank the house.

Brick came up beside him as they approached the door. They weren't small men. He mouthed the count of three, then they both rammed the door with the sides of their bodies. It took two firm strikes, then it flew back against the wall with a crack.

The lights were out and Brick nearly tripped over

a body in the foyer. He aimed a small flashlight on the floor. It wasn't one of theirs. He wasn't sure if that was good or bad considering how quiet the house was.

"Skull Nation," Brick whispered.

They proceeded deeper into the house. The glow from oven light highlighted another body, but this one started moving as they entered, so he instinctively drew his gun.

"Boss…"

He dropped down to one knee. It was Tank, his hands clutching his stomach. There was fucking blood everywhere. "What happened?"

"Skull Nation. They're out back. The barn…"

"Shit! You're going be fine, Tank. Hang on."

Tank was one of the biggest guys in the club. A real force. He'd single-handedly gotten them out of a lot of scrapes with his sheer size and strength. As much as he wanted to call for backup or get him to a doctor right away, he had to clear this scene and find his woman first.

The party was apparently outside in the barn. If they'd put one hand on Ally, he'd kill them all nice and slow. They met up with the other brothers out back. Reaper had an automatic across his chest. The spotlight in the rear alley gave them a wash of light to see by.

He heard a scuffle coming from the barn, followed by breaking glass, so they all broke into a run. So many scenarios ran through his head. What if Ally was already dead? What if they'd tortured her? Raped her?

The Skull Nation was capable of anything.

Bullets rang out close to his ear. He hadn't even seen the threat before Tarmac began firing beside him. Lord saw the opposing muzzle flash coming from the side of the barn. They scattered, firing back. The darkness and deafening gunfire created an atmosphere of pure chaos. He didn't even know where Ally had been taken.

"Watch where you're shooting," he shouted out to his men. He ran in a crouch, getting as close to the barn as possible. With a forward kick, the old wooden door planks broke apart. A lone lightbulb hung from the ceiling of the barn, swinging back and forth from the commotion.

"Lord, in the first stall." It was Rancher. He was on the ground, a gun in his hand as he covered him from the Skull Nation. Stump was behind a wall of hay bales, leaning to the side to fire deeper into the barn. Lord rushed over to join him.

"Where's Ally?" he shouted to be heard.

"Don't know. We got here and the Skull Nation fired on us as soon as we pulled up."

"Fuck," Lord muttered. She was probably already dead. Dread and panic consumed him. "We need to finish this. Tank's bleeding out in the house."

They took a breath and charged into the barn with guns blazing. His other men followed, creating a line of fire. Nothing could survive that much lead.

When it didn't seem they were being fired at, he stopped shooting.

"Stop!" he called out.

Silence.

"Brick, check it out. Make sure they're all dead," Lord said. He went to check on Rancher. "Where are the women and kids?"

Gunpowder still lingered in the air, creating a fog similar to a battlefield. Rancher's leg was shot up. He couldn't move. Without medical help, he'd bleed out the same as Tank.

"I never made it to the house," he said. Then he swallowed hard before continuing. "I heard Ally calling for help, but those fuckers had already surrounded the house. I couldn't get to her."

"Called from the house?"

He nodded.

Lord clapped his old friend on the shoulder before rushing off. They'd controlled the scene, but what about the house? There had been a body by the door and Tank had been shot in the kitchen. He didn't want to find Ally's body.

Reaper ran with him. They did a sweep of the main floor. Tank was still holding on, but he didn't look good.

"Call the club. Get a truck here with a doctor. Right fucking now," Lord told Reaper before taking the stairs alone. As he burst into room after room, he heard a muffled cry coming from the end of the hall.

Lord stopped dead.

He slowly neared the door. Judging by the location, it had to be the room he saw from the street, the one where the light had turned off as he'd approached the house. He took measured breaths, but the squeaky wooden floorboards gave him away. Gunfire sprayed the door, but he kept out of the line of fire. There was at least one Skull Nation motherfucker still breathing. He couldn't give him more time if he had a hostage. Whether he lived or died, he had to end this now.

****

Ally kept hugging her stomach, hoping to somehow protect her unborn baby from harm. After the firefight outside ended, she began to lose hope again. But the prez of the Skull Nation was firing at something now, so that meant whoever was on the other side of the door was on their side. If it was Lord, she prayed he wasn't hit by all the gunfire.

"Don't fucking breathe," he whispered in

143

warning. He had a gunshot wound to the side of his body and hadn't been doing too well in the last twenty minutes or so. The skin of his face had blanched unnaturally white. Betty's first and only shot had done the damage, but they didn't even realize until after he'd nearly knocked them both out. He'd tied Betty's wrists to the sink leg and he had a rope around Ally's neck, the other end firmly in his fist. Whenever she whined or squirmed, he'd tug it hard enough to steal her air.

There was a bang on the bathroom door, making the prez panic and spray the door with bullets again. She shielded her head and face from the splinters of wood. As soon as he stopped firing, what was left of the door burst open. He yanked her leash tight, pulling her in front of him as a shield.

It was Lord.

She felt her entire body melt and her knees gave out completely. He was a beautiful sight. Before the prez could react, Lord moved impossibly fast, lunging forward and wrapping his hand around the man's neck. He slammed his head against the wall with force. The medicine cabinet crashed down into the sink. Betty shielded her head. With Ally's rope on the ground, she quickly crawled over to untie Betty.

"You have my woman tied up like a fucking dog?" Lord rammed his head into the wall over and over, the sounds sickening. Some of the brothers from the club appeared in the doorway, but they didn't move to interfere.

Ally was worried about Rancher and the kids. Seeing Lord in the flesh felt almost like a dream after the night she'd had. He'd found her. Saved her.

She sat on the floor with Betty, keeping her eyes averted as Lord literally beat the man to death. He was a powerhouse, an unrelenting beast of vengeance. All she could see in her peripheral vision was red.

When everything went quiet, Betty nudged her. She looked over and saw Lord covered in blood. He looked like the devil himself. But he wasn't, she knew that more than anyone.

After wiping his hands on his jeans, he beckoned her to stand. She was hesitant. They'd been kept prisoners in the bathroom since this attack started. The prez had wanted to kill her in front of Lord, so he could watch him suffer.

"I'm so sorry, baby." He pulled her close and she tried to ignore all the blood and accept the comfort. "Did he touch you?"

"No."

"You were right. I never should have left you behind."

"I wasn't sure if you'd come."

"I'll always come for you, Ally." He pressed his forehead to hers, and despite their circumstances, she could feel the love and intimacy from the simple act. They had each other back.

"Where's Rancher?" asked Betty.

"He's in the barn. The doctor's probably here by now. He's shot in the leg," Lord said. Betty rushed out the bathroom door. She heard the footfalls all the way down the stairs.

"I thought I was dead. Thought I'd never see you again," she said.

"I'll take good care of you." As he led her out of the bathroom, his men parted for them. They were heavily armed and she finally felt safe that the club had come. At the bottom of the stairs, she saw Betty reunite with her kids before heading out back. They'd been excellent, staying in their secret place without a noise the entire time.

"Should we stay?" she asked.

He shook his head. Lord looked exhausted. "We'll check in tomorrow. I'll leave a couple guys here tonight on watch, just in case."

She didn't argue. All she wanted to do was get back to the club, take a shower, and sleep for a week. He held her hand as they walked out to his bike in the darkness. The air was crisp at this time of night, soothing after being holed up in the small bathroom. It had been too claustrophobic for her liking.

"Will it always be like this?" she asked.

He mounted the bike and helped her climb on behind him. "Like what?"

"Knowing I can lose you every time you ride away."

Lord leaned back in his seat enough so they could kiss. It was a soft, gentle kiss. "This is over now. We learn from our mistakes, and from now on you stay by my side."

"Good. That's where I want to be."

The bike was kicked to life, and the familiar rumble of the engine reminded her of Lord. Together, they rode back to the club with some of his men behind them. She held him tight around the waist, feeling safe and relieved to be heading home. The nightmare was over and, as far as she knew, no Straight to Hell men had been killed.

As they approached, the gates were opened for them. They all filed in, and the gates were securely closed behind them. She'd hated this place when Lord had brought her here, but now it was her sanctuary.

After parking, Lord didn't help her off the bike. Instead, he swung her body up into his arms and carried her inside to their bedroom. His strength always amazed her … and turned her on.

"Tonight, we need to wash off every memory of this fucked-up day. Then we'll sleep long and hard," Lord said.

"And tomorrow?"

"Tomorrow I'll show you exactly how grateful I am to have you back."

****

One week later

Lord left Tank's room when the doctor came in to check on him. His surgery had gone well last week. He'd have a nasty scar on his stomach, but he'd heal as good as new.

Rancher would need to be off his feet for a while, but Betty was more than happy to wait on him and keep things running on their ranch. The club covered the cost of all the damages.

As far as they knew, all senior members of the Skull Nation had been wiped out. If there were any others, they'd gone into hiding … for now. They'd play it safe for a while longer, but Lord was confident this war was over.

"How's he doing?" asked Brick once Lord was in the hallway.

"He's a tough motherfucker. You'd think he cut himself shaving."

"Good. How's your girl? Still shaken up?"

Lord shook his head. "She's tough, too."

"Tough enough to be your old lady?" Brick raised an eyebrow.

"I'm not even going to answer that." Lord kept walking toward his room. Before opening the door, he turned to his VP. "I'm making it official tonight."

"About time."

Once inside the room, Ally rushed him. He

twirled her around, then held her close. "You're happy today. Feeling better?" Yesterday, she'd been sick in the morning. He blamed the cookout they'd had the previous night. Probably undercooked meat.

"I need to talk to you about something."

"Can it wait?" He didn't want to deal with problems today. Didn't want to talk more about the attack again. Now that things around the club were finally shifting back to normal, he wanted to lower his guard enough to enjoy his woman. "I have some unfinished business."

"Are you leaving?" Ally balled his shirt up in her fists.

He began to walk her backward. She kept her hands on his chest. "This business can be handled right here."

She was about to question him but stopped when he leaned down to kiss her neck. He trailed kisses along her skin before suckling her earlobe into his mouth. She let out a little moan.

"This business I can handle," she whispered close to his lips.

"You're the best thing to ever happen to me, Ally."

"I love you, Lord."

They kissed, hard and demanding. The connection between the two of them was always simmering. He couldn't even imagine how life would be if he'd lost her last week. Nothing would get between them again. He'd learned from his mistakes. The safest place for his old lady was at the club and by his side.

"Let me see my beautiful body," he said.

A barely-there smile appeared on her lips. She slipped out of her pants and tugged off her shirt. Her long blonde hair fanned out along her bare back.

"No bra again?"

She shook her head.

He loved the way those big tits sloped out into tempting peaks. Her body was lush and he'd never get tired of fucking the same woman for the rest of this life. He was addicted to Ally.

"Lose those panties before I rip them off."

She wiggled out of them, staring at him the entire time.

"Are you wet for me? You should always be wet for your man, Ally."

When she didn't attempt to answer, he pulled her close to his body. He reached low and impaled her pussy with two fingers. She was hot and slick, making his cock even harder. He pushed in with his fingers until he was knuckles deep. She gasped, wrapping her arms around his neck.

"I need you, Lord."

"You want my cock, baby girl?"

He toyed with her G-spot, increasing her arousal. Her eyes became hooded and she dropped lower, trying to get more of his fingers.

"Please…"

"Get on your knees. I want to watch your mouth wrapped around my dick, Ally."

She bit her lower lip but did as told.

Once she was on her knees, he unbuckled his pants, then unzipped. His erection was thick and ready. She didn't hesitate, grabbing the base and bringing it to her mouth.

As soon as her lips covered the swollen head, he groaned aloud. It felt so fucking amazing. The image of his girl taking his cock was the most beautiful sight. She sucked him so damn good, her head bobbing over his length with vigor.

"Good girl."

He wrapped his fist in her long, blonde hair, guiding her deeper. She was gorgeous. Lord savored the way she sucked and licked, careful not to use her teeth. But he was getting too close and didn't want to come down her throat.

If he wanted to make a family with her, he needed to make sure to come deep in her cunt every time they fucked. Besides, no way would he leave his woman unsatisfied.

He tugged her head back and she squeaked from the bite of her hair being pulled. Her lips were swollen and red, her eyes filled with need.

"I want your pussy, baby," he said. "Get on the bed and spread your legs for me. I'll take you heaven."

She slowly crawled onto the bed. His modest little virgin had turned into a vixen, teasing him every chance she got. He loved her full, round ass and the way her tits swayed when she was on all fours. Within minutes, she was in the middle of the bed, her legs spread open in invitation. Her pink pussy glistened. He pushed down his cock to no avail, but he ignored his needs and sank down on his stomach.

Lord slid his hands under her ass, getting comfortable. He loved eating Ally's pussy. He started by licking her in long, firm strokes, over and over, savoring her. She began to writhe, begging for more.

He settled over her clit, sucking her until she was panting, her pussy spasming erratically. She clutched the sheets, arching up against his mouth.

"Lord, I want you inside me when I come."

That was one request he couldn't deny, especially when he was so close to blowing his load. He rose to his knees, taking off his shirt. She watched every move.

When he lowered between her legs, her little

hands were all over him, squeezing his muscles and clawing at his back. She drove him crazy. He poised at her entrance, teasing her until she begged him to fuck her. Then he thrust in deep, filling her to the hilt.

She tossed her head back and moaned like a whore—his whore. He pumped his hips, driving into her over and over. She was hot and tight around his dick, both their bodies slick from clean sweat.

Every time they were together, it was a mix of passion, making love, and hard-core fucking. She was perfect in every way.

He couldn't take any more. "Come for me, Ally. Come all over my dick." He picked up the tempo, taking her harder and faster until she couldn't help but comply. She panted with each thrust. The moment she let go and spasmed around his cock, he came inside her, filling her with his seed.

It took a while to come down from the high. He stayed inside her, holding his weight off her body before finally sliding off to the side. She crawled up his chest, getting comfortable in the crook of his arm.

"I like this," he said. "You belong right beside me."

"Lord?"

"What, baby." He was still winded.

"Remember I needed to talk about something? Well, I'm not sure how you'll take it."

He narrowed his eyes as he turned to look at her. "What did you do?"

"Nothing. It's more what you did to me," she said. "I'm pregnant, Lord."

He hated that she looked nervous as hell, as if it would piss him off she carried his child.

He shifted to his side, propped up on an elbow. "You're sure?"

She nodded. "I used a test at Rancher's place."

"Why you just telling me now?"

"I didn't want to add to the list of problems," she said.

"Baby, this is no fucking problem. You're making a baby. Our baby. There's nothing better than that."

"Really?"

He kissed her lips, completely enamored by his woman. A child was a new beginning, a chance for him to live vicariously through a brand new little human. His childhood was a shitshow, but their son or daughter would only know peace and love.

"I've never been happier, Ally. Not a single day in my life. You've changed my world completely."

She ran her fingers along his face, carefully touching his scars. "And to think you were going to kill me."

He smirked. "And here I am, putty in your hands."

"I love you, Lord."

"I love you, baby."

The End

www.samcrescent.com

www.staceyespino.com

EVERNIGHT PUBLISHING ®

www.evernightpublishing.com